A Baker's Heart

Crawdad Beach Series (Book 4)

Lisa Buffaloe

A Baker's Heart
John 15:11 Publications
Copyright 2024 Lisa Brewer Buffaloe
All rights reserved.

Artificial Intelligence was not used in writing this book. This novel is a work of fiction. Names, characters, places, towns, bakeries, bakery owners, Cybersecurity specialists, software security specialists, business owners, ethical hackers, crawdads, and all people and incidents are the product of the author's active imagination and are used fictitiously. Any resemblance to actual events, persons living or dead, or any other person, including any place or thing, is entirely coincidental and beyond the author's intent. No crawdads were hurt in the making of this novel.

Visit the author's website at https://lisabuffaloe.com.

ISBN: 978-1-957715-23-0 (eBook)
ISBN: 978-1-957715-24-7 (Paperback)
ISBN: 978-1-957715-25-4 (Hardcover)

Cover Design: Lisa Buffaloe. Cupcake Photo: Debbie Ryan (debbieryan2009, Pixabay). Original Dough photo: Daniel (dni2012 Pixabay)

A Baker's Heart

Olivia Baker left behind her cheating boyfriend and her career as a pastry chef in one of the finest restaurants in Houston. Arriving in the quirky town of Crawdad Beach, Olivia is given the incredible gift of starting her own bakery and living a dream come true. However, gifts and blessings haven't stopped her anger at God or fixed her wounded heart.

Cybersecurity expert Marcus Patterson is grateful his job keeps him busy and out of trouble. However, his culinary incompetence puts him at risk when he hires the town's new baker as his personal chef. Marcus knows how to stop a computer hacker, but he's not sure he can handle the temptation Olivia brings.

Will their friendship cook up love or be a recipe for disaster?

...

Table of Contents

Chapter 1

The only steamy thing in her life was her bakery oven.

Olivia Baker sighed as she collapsed on her apartment couch. Maybe someday she'd meet a decent guy, but she wasn't ready to date again after the disastrous relationship she'd left in Texas.

She glanced around the beautiful loft apartment at the high ceilings, brick walls, hardwood floors, fireplace, and French doors leading to a balcony overlooking downtown Crawdad Beach. Her Aunt Katherine had done a great job renovating the old building. Plus, Olivia had been given free rein to design the downstairs for the soon-to-be-opened bakery she'd named *Rolling in the Dough.*

Crossing to the French doors, Olivia peeked out of the blinds. Streetlights cast the brick-paved Main Street in a pretty glow. All was quiet.

Most of the old two-story brick buildings had stayed in use over the years or had been renovated. The town's sense of humor showed with the names of several businesses, including Knick Knacks Antiques, Curl and Dye Beauty Salon, Doohickeys Hardware, and Tiddlywinks Restaurant. Even the town's name was amusing since Crawdad Beach wasn't on the beach. A small boy with the first settlers suggested the name when he noticed a crawdad sunning on the sandy riverbank.

Living in a small town was different than her hometown of Houston. There were a few things Olivia missed about the big city, but here, she had an abundance of family members. She'd already hired a full-time employee to help with the bakery. They already had several taste testings of their pastries, and everyone seemed to love what they had baked.

As excited as Olivia was about the incredible opportunity her grandad had given her to be the building's owner, she hesitated to set a date for the bakery's grand opening since her mom, Crystal, needed another surgery.

Olivia went to her bedroom and sat on the edge of her bed. Crystal kept telling Olivia to trust God, enjoy life, and open the bakery. But how was she supposed to enjoy life when her mom needed another surgery?

Olivia sighed. How on earth could she trust God when all her prayers for healing for her dad's cancer had not been answered?

Not again! His smoke alarm blaring, Marcus Patterson groaned, pushed back from his desk, and rushed to his apartment kitchen. Taking the smoldering pot of burning ramen off the stove, he set it in the sink and drowned the mess in water. Marcus turned on the fan over the stove. No matter what he tried to cook, he seemed to have the skill of burning almost everything. His guardian angel probably got hazard pay.

To air out the place, he opened the balcony French doors and hurried back to his computer. Between working for Dustin Bowman's software security firm, Marcus also worked for a few high-profile individuals needing a cybersecurity computer specialist.

Hordes of hackers were out there, causing havoc all over the world. If only he could clone himself, he'd sit at his computer, have a clone to cook meals, and another clone to take over when he needed to sleep.

Marcus checked the time. Tomorrow afternoon, he was scheduled to help install security software for the new bakery. Besides the beautiful owner, part of the deal was that she had agreed to cook him a meal after he finished. The thought of a non-burnt meal had his stomach growling.

Ignoring his hunger pains, he went back to battle. Even if it took all night, he had to stop the cyber-attack.

Chapter 2

His clean scent tantalizing her senses, Olivia stood in the bakery office behind Marcus. He seemed oblivious to her presence as his fingers flew across the computer keyboard.

Olivia tapped his shoulder. "The meal is almost finished."

Marcus didn't look up. "Great. I have about five more minutes, and I'll be done."

"Thanks again for installing the security software."

"My pleasure. It's nice to get out of my apartment."

"Do you do all your work there?"

He held up his hand and leaned closer to the computer screen before giving her a quick glance. "Sorry, I had to check something. For the most part, I'm at home. I do go into the main office at times. But since that is only a few buildings away, it's not like I have much of a social life."

Olivia was stunned by that statement. His tanned skin, dark hair, and black-rimmed glasses gave him an intellectual but very attractive look. She would have thought he would have a date every night. "You don't take time for yourself?"

Marcus continued working and shrugged. "I see my sister Alexa and her family now and then."

"What do you do for fun?"

He stopped typing and looked at her like she was an alien. "Fun? Oh," Behind his glasses, his brown eyes blinked a few times. "I like computers. My job is challenging, yet enjoyable." His gaze returned to what he was doing.

"Okay. If you don't need me, just come upstairs when you finish."

He gave her a nod.

Feeling dismissed, Olivia went upstairs to her apartment kitchen. The table was set, and she'd made Chicken Cordon Bleu, a salad, and homemade rolls. For dessert, she'd made a Sacher Torte, which just happened to be her favorite decadent dark chocolate treat.

She loved baking and cooking, and Marcus seemed to love what he did. She couldn't imagine sitting behind a computer all day. At least with baking, she was moving around the kitchen.

Olivia checked the oven. Everything was ready. Setting the oven on warm, she returned downstairs.

Marcus clicked on the computer mouse as pages and information flew across the screen. "I think I've got you safe now."

Olivia peeked over his shoulder. "Is there anything I

need to know about the software?"

"Nope. It should happily run in the background and protect your computer from problems. If you'd like, I can monitor everything for you on my server back at my apartment. I'd need your permission for that, though."

"That would be great. I don't know anything about computer software."

Marcus nodded and typed again on the keyboard. "Okay, give me a few minutes, and I'll take care of that for you."

"How much do I owe you for all of this?"

His fingers stopped typing, and he glanced up at her. "You're cooking dinner, right?"

"Yes."

"Okay, then I'm good." His gaze returned to the computer screen, and he returned to work.

"Really? That's all you want?"

"You know cooking is an issue for me, so you providing a meal is a huge blessing."

"You're easy to please."

He grinned up at her, reminding her of a little boy about to be given a bowl of his favorite ice cream.

Heat rose up her back, and she stepped away from him. "I'll be upstairs when you finish." Behind his brown-eyed gaze, she sensed he could be a real temptation, and she did not need temptations.

Olivia waited for him in the kitchen. She needed to

keep her heart safely closed, locked, and protected.

She didn't hear him come up the stairs; just caught a sniff of his clean scent. Trying to act nonchalant, Olivia glanced over her shoulder. "You ready to eat?"

Marcus grinned. "Yes, please."

Turning her back to him, she opened the oven and took out the meal. Thankfully, it hadn't dried out while she waited for him to finish.

He helped her carry the dishes she had prepared. "This smells and looks amazing." He set them in the middle of the table, then hurried to pull her chair out and waited until she sat.

Olivia thanked him. Her old boyfriend never had done that for her.

Sitting in his chair, Marcus looked her way. "Mind if I pray?"

Surprised. she shrugged. "No, that's fine." Praying was what her mom and grandad did, not her.

Marcus lowered his head and prayed a sweet prayer that included her. Looking up, he picked up his fork. "I can't thank you enough for doing this for me."

"You haven't even started eating."

"My meals have never looked or smelled this good." Besides the groans of pleasure, he ate in silence. Marcus looked her way. "Oh man, this is the best meal I've ever had."

Olivia grinned at his comment. "I would be extremely

flattered at your kind words if you weren't the guy who burned ramen noodles."

He chewed his food, then swallowed. "I'm serious. You are an amazing cook. Or should I say chef extraordinaire?"

She liked how that sounded. "I'm a trained pastry chef and know how to cook other things."

"Well, whatever your training, you are amazing. I can't wait until you open the bakery. Of course, I may have to spend more time working out."

His chest already seemed well-defined and muscular. The way he looked, he probably had six-pack abs. When her gaze roamed back to his face, he was smiling.

Behind his glasses, his cocoa-brown eyes held her entranced as he leaned toward her. "I'm a software security computer geek but have a good exercise regimen."

Her cheeks heated, and she looked away. Marcus was definitely someone she would love spending more time with. What was she thinking? She barely knew the guy and didn't need a relationship; she had a business to run. However, having a male friend would be nice. But the thoughts she had about Marcus went far beyond the friendship level.

He held up his fork and pointed it at her. "I have a proposition for you."

She tried not to choke on the bite she was eating.

"What?"

His eyes widened, and he held up his hand in apology. "Sorry. That did not sound appropriate. Let me rephrase. Would you be willing to be my private chef? I'd love to have you every evening." His face flamed red. "I mean. I'd love to have your cooking every day, but I'd settle for anything from one to seven days a week. I'd pay you for the food and services. I mean, for your cooking." He clamped his mouth shut and sighed. "Sorry."

Olivia stifled a giggle at his obvious discomfort. Could she even consider something like that? Once the bakery opened, how much time would she have? As it stood now, she planned on opening early and closing around three o'clock.

Maybe after she closed the bakery, she could cook something for him in her apartment. That way, she could drop it off and return to her place. As much as she enjoyed being around him, she already did not trust herself to be alone with him every day of the week.

Marcus gave her an apologetic look. "Hey, I'm sorry. I shouldn't have asked you. I know you're going to be running a business. You don't need to worry about me. I probably should just order food from Tiddlywinks. They're the best restaurant around, actually the only restaurant in town, but it would still be nice to have something cooked by you. Because you're great." He closed his eyes and shook his head. "I should just eat and stop talking. But maybe we could try it for a week or so, and if it became too much for you, you could just let me know. Or, we could forget it. You're a great cook. I like you. I mean, I don't know you that well, but still, I appreciate you feeding me." He sighed, hung his head, and returned to eating.

She muted her laugh with a cough. Did the poor guy never get to talk to people while working on the computer? Spending time with Marcus could be enjoyable, and he did seem to need a healthy meal and probably some company. Maybe she could at least help him out for a few weeks. "Okay, we can try."

His head jerked up. "Great. I know your Aunt Katherine will be pleased I won't be trying to cook. She did a great job renovating the building into loft apartments and would probably appreciate me not setting off the smoke alarms and smoking up the place. So, how about two hundred dollars a week plus whatever food costs you have?"

"That would be more than generous."

"I know it would add to your responsibilities, and I don't want to take advantage of you."

Olivia tried to hide her grin but just couldn't.

Marcus blew out a long sigh. "I am really messing this up. I'm much better with computers."

"You're doing fine. Tell you what, I will cook your meals. One a day. For a week. If it gets too difficult, I'll step back as long as it wouldn't hurt being your friend if I have to quit."

He held out his hand. "Friends with or without meals." He gave her hand a firm shake. "Thanks, Olivia."

She returned his smile. "I have one other request."

"Name it. I'm yours."

Ignoring that little tidbit he offered, she changed the subject. "Want to be my taste tester for some new desserts?"

"I would love that. Really love that. Thank you. Bless you. I'm salivating just thinking about it." He wiped his mouth with his napkin and gave her a broad smile.

After dinner, he helped her clean the kitchen, and they sat together on the couch. Much to her surprise, Marcus freely shared about his childhood and some of the crazy things he and his sister, Alexa, did when they were growing up. His mom was born and raised in Puerto Vallarta, which must have been where Marcus got his very attractive Latin look. His dad was involved in the government. Olivia assumed it was the United States, but she hadn't asked, and Marcus didn't share details. He mentioned that his occupation choice started with a government job before he went to the private sector.

When Marcus told her his faith was important, Olivia quickly changed the subject and gave only a few details about her background. She didn't need pity about her dad's death and didn't need to be judged for how she had lived her life with her past boyfriend. Marcus didn't pry, but he did seem to notice and even sat still as though studying her for a moment. She had squirmed under his scrutiny. Shortly after that, he thanked her and left.

Olivia sunk into the cushions of the couch. Marcus was handsome, personable, intelligent, six years older than she, and very friendly. She liked men more stable than most guys her age, but she didn't need a guy in her life. And Marcus was probably too nice for her.

She would cook his meals, which meant she would see him almost every evening. Olivia shoved a strand of hair behind her ear. Why had she agreed to that? She had enough to do with getting the bakery ready to open.

But how could she not think about Marcus's dark chocolate eyes that had surveyed her with interest but never with a look of lust. It wasn't like Marcus was giving off vibes that he wanted to date her, but something drew her toward him. Not in a bad way, but more of a curiosity.

Even when the conversation had gone uncomfortable when he talked about his faith, he didn't look at her like he was judging her. His expression had been different, and she couldn't place it. Compassion? Concern? Gentleness? It wasn't just that he was handsome and nice; something inside him seemed to pull her toward him.

Olivia shoved off the couch and went to her bedroom. She needed to read a book, watch television, and do something other than think about Marcus.

Chapter 3

"How did things go with Marcus last night?"

Ignoring Jennifer's hopeful grin, Olivia shrugged and returned to making a new recipe for the bakery. "Marcus installed the software. I cooked him dinner, and we talked. He had an interesting childhood since his dad was involved with the government. Sounds like spy stuff."

Jennifer raised an eyebrow. "His sister, Alexa, has the energy of a hyper-hummingbird. Does Marcus move around at high speed, too?"

"Alexa is the one who has that lightning bolt shaved in her hair from when she was a track star, right?" At Jennifer's nod, Olivia continued. "Marcus seems pretty normal speed, other than when he's typing on the computer keyboard. Plus, he was a complete gentleman, which means you and my mom would approve of him."

Jennifer smiled as she rolled out pastry dough to make cinnamon rolls. "Marcus would come in Tiddlywinks sometimes to get a meal. I waited on him a few times, and he was really nice. Are you going to see him again?"

Olivia's heartbeat cranked up at the thought of the handsome man. She tried to act nonchalant. "Yeah, later tonight."

Jennifer stopped what she was doing and stared at her. "Really? How exciting."

"No. It's just that the poor guy has no cooking skills, and someone has to help him. He asked me to consider cooking his meals for him."

"He did?" Jennifer waggled her eyebrows. "My, my, my. That sounds promising."

Olivia rolled her eyes at her friend's excitement. "It's just a business deal if I do it."

"Will you have time for that?"

"I don't know. I'll see how it goes." Olivia still wasn't sure why she was cooking meals for Marcus when she had so many things to consider with the bakery. But, she did enjoy baking and cooking meals. Plus, she needed to eat something herself. What better way to make sure she ate healthy? And seeing a great-looking guy would be an excellent way to end her day.

The oven timer dinged, and Olivia removed a sheet of baked cookies and laid them on the stainless steel prep table. The smell made her mouth water. Soon, her bakery's glass cases would be filled with all kinds of delectable creations.

Jennifer sprinkled cinnamon and sugar on her prepared dough. "I heard Chester and your granddad checked Marcus out when he first moved to town."

"I heard about that. That's so funny."

"I think it's sweet. People here take care of one another."

Olivia blew on a cookie to cool it down, then popped a bite in her mouth. It was good, really good. She'd text her family to stop by this afternoon to check out the day's creations. Several female family members were planning on helping once the bakery opened.

Trying to avoid continuing to discuss the very handsome Marcus, Olivia lobbed a question back at Jennifer. "Do you miss waitressing at Tiddlywinks?"

"Yeah, it was fun to interact with so many people," Jennifer grinned as she looked around the kitchen, "but working in a bakery has always been my dream."

Olivia nodded. "It is pretty cool, huh?"

"Oh, it is. When I was little, my mom let me cook fun things in the kitchen."

"My mom did, too. Poor dad was brave enough to try all sorts of interesting combinations." Thinking about her father, Olivia felt the familiar sadness and hurt morphing into anger. *Why did God take her dad?* Olivia placed the still-warm cookies on a decorative plate and then took the cookie sheet to the sink to wash.

"Have you thought about when you want to open the bakery?"

Olivia forced her attention back to Jennifer. "I don't know. We're ready, but I'm still worried about my mom." The surgeon had removed a softball-sized benign tumor from her thigh, but her mom still had a tear in her hip socket and torn tendons on the outside of her hip.

"I understand. Does Crystal have a date set for her next surgery?"

"Not yet. Between getting married and healing from having that tumor removed, Mom is waiting."

"Well, the CBPT is praying for her," Jennifer said.

"CBPT?"

"Yeah, the Crawdad Beach Prayer Team."

"That's right." Olivia nodded. "Mom mentioned something about them."

"It's like the town has a prayer covering."

"Must be nice." Olivia half-listened as Jennifer went on to talk about God and her faith, not in a pushy way; it was just part of who she was. Probably because she hadn't had anything bad happen in her life. Olivia grimaced at that thought because she knew that wasn't true. Many people had terrible things happen to them but still loved God and were faithful in following Him. She'd been like that before her dad had died. But she'd gotten so angry she'd pushed God out of her life.

Olivia shoved her hands in the sink's soapy dishwater. Sometimes, she missed having a God connection. But how could she, and would she, ever get moving back in that direction?

After stopping the cyber-attack, Marcus used his company name to type out an invoice to send to his client. Very few knew that Marcus was the owner and single employee who handled cybersecurity for several high-profile people.

Although Marcus had left Los Angeles, unfortunately, he still hadn't finished cutting ties with everyone from his past. God had graciously rescued him from his partying lifestyle with Hollywood celebrities. He truly thanked God that there weren't any photos or videos of him on social media during that time.

His sister had convinced him to move to Crawdad Beach, where temptation would not be as big a problem. Alexa had been correct; no wild parties or A-list celebrities were here in this little town, which made it a perfect place for him to stay busy and out of trouble.

Marcus sat up straighter. He was proud of himself for cleaning up his act. He corrected his thought; he was grateful that God graciously helped him get his focus back on track. He felt and looked better, and his mind was more at peace than it had been in years.

The only thing that unsettled him now was that later today, he would be with the tall, slim, beautiful baker with light brown hair and big brown eyes who didn't seem to share his faith.

Marcus blew out a breath. He hoped and prayed he

would positively influence Olivia and wouldn't get into something he would regret.

Chapter 4

At five-thirty in the evening, Olivia stood outside Marcus's apartment building. With her hands full, she wasn't sure how she would open the door. To top it off, it started to drizzle with just enough misty rain to probably make her hair frizz.

Since Marcus only lived a few buildings away from the bakery, she hadn't considered she might need a carry sack to deliver his food. She maneuvered and adjusted her dishes and still couldn't get a hand free.

"Let me help." Her granddad's best friend, Chester, opened the door for her and sniffed. "Sure smells good." The older man grinned as he motioned with his chin toward the stairs. "You wouldn't be taking that to a certain young man who is a computer geek, would you?"

"Maybe."

Chester chuckled. "Your secret is safe with me. Don't worry, I like Marcus."

She curbed her smile as she glanced his way. "Yeah, I heard about you and Grandad checking out the new guys who move to town."

Chester's mischievous grin lit his face. "Well, we must

ensure we keep you young ladies safe." He tipped his head. "Have a nice evening, Olivia."

"You, too." She made her way up the stairs but still didn't have a free hand, so she used her foot to knock on Marcus's apartment door. She waited a few minutes, but there was no response. *Great*. Was Marcus even home? She kicked a little harder.

The door swung open. Marcus, wearing jeans and a dark green polo shirt, stood there, blinking at her as though she had materialized out of thin air. He shook his head. "Sorry, I'm in the middle of something. Please come in." He stepped aside to let her in, then closed the door behind her. "I'll be right back." He rushed away and disappeared through a door off the family room.

Olivia stared at his sparsely furnished den with a brown leather couch, one leather chair, a large-screen television, and a coffee table. He had nothing personal, not even a picture on the wall or the fireplace mantle.

Since he hadn't returned, she walked to the kitchen and placed her dishes on his counter. Should she wait, go, or should she set the table? Maybe having everything ready whenever he came out would be good.

She rummaged through his cabinets and drawers, looking for plates, glasses, and silverware. Good grief, her guy friends in college had more dishes than Marcus. At least he had a small table where he could eat.

Once finished, Olivia considered leaving. Since

Marcus was still in the other room, she turned on his oven to keep the food warm. Should she let herself out the door or go find him?

Maybe he wanted her to bring his food where he worked? She took hesitant steps and peered inside the open door. The room looked like command central at a government facility. A bank of computer monitors covered the walls with data scrolling by like a sci-fi movie.

Marcus muttered something under his breath as he typed in rapid speed. "Oh, no, you don't."

Olivia froze. "I'm sorry."

Marcus whipped his head around, blinked a few times as he blankly stared at her. "No, not you. I'm trying to get rid of this cyber-creep." He returned to typing, then sat still. Several screens went blank. He pumped his fist in the air. "Got him! Take that, you evil cyber-monster!" Turning in his chair, he gave her a big smile. "Hi, Olivia."

Olivia shook her head, wondering where the intense computer guy had gone. "Hi."

He stood. "So, what did you bring for dinner?" He motioned for her to go in front of him and followed her to the kitchen.

Olivia opened the oven. "For your dining pleasure, I have shrimp rémoulade, hearts of romaine, boiled potatoes, and vegetables. Dessert is a Meyer Lemon Tarte topped with honey-kissed toasted meringue and raspberries."

Marcus laid a hand on his chest. "That sounds amazing. I am not paying you enough money for meals like this." He took out his wallet and handed her a hundred-dollar bill.

She chuckled and backed away. "That's not necessary."

Marcus shoved the money in her hand. "No, really, take this. You have no idea how much this makes me happy. I haven't eaten like this since..." He looked away for a few seconds. "Anyway, come on, won't you join me?"

"No, I made the meal for you." Olivia removed the food from the oven and set it on the table.

He stood beside her. "But eating is more fun with a friend."

She couldn't believe she hadn't kept a portion back at her place because it smelled so good. "I probably should go home."

"I'd prefer your company. Eating alone is no fun." Marcus dipped his head, trying to catch her attention. "Please?" He pulled out a chair for her and waited.

How could she say no to such a handsome face? "Okay. Fine." Her mouth watering, she settled in the seat, watching as he sat across from her.

"Thanks for the meal, and thank you for staying." He held his hand out toward her. "Mind if I pray?"

She hesitated only a moment, then took his hand.

He bowed his head and prayed, thanking God for the

meal and for her. Olivia's throat tightened. His words made her feel like she had been wrapped in a warm hug.

Finished with praying, Marcus squeezed her fingers and released her hand. "Thanks again. I'm glad you stayed. I've been looking forward to this meal all day." He took a bite and moaned in pleasure. "I can't believe you don't have an army camped outside your door begging you to cook their meals."

She chuckled. "Not hardly. I'm used to being in the kitchen away from clients. The main chef at the restaurant where I used to work got all the glory." Her stomach churned at the thought of her ex-boyfriend. "I was just a pastry chef."

"*Just* a pastry chef?" Marcus looked like she was crazy. "That's a big deal, and the fact you can cook like a five-star chef is incredible." He chewed another bite with a look of pure satisfaction on his face. "Mmm."

Well, at least someone appreciated her achievements. "Thanks. So, do you get kudos for the job you do?"

"Not really. I'm more of a behind-the-scenes guy."

"Do you like that?"

Marcus took his time answering. "Yeah, I do. Most people don't realize how many jobs are out of the public eye."

"I guess that's true. But, are you okay being so isolated?"

He chewed as he stared at his plate for a moment. "I

don't know. I have friends."

She grinned. "Online or in person?"

"Most are online and a few in person."

"Do you date?" She crammed a bite into her mouth and stared at the food in front of her. Even though she was curious, she shouldn't have asked that question.

Marcus took off his glasses and rubbed the bridge of his nose. His eyelashes were almost longer than hers. "Yeah, I've dated." The tone of his voice said more than his words as if it had not been a pleasant experience. His gaze slid to her. "How about you?"

Olivia smoothed the napkin in her lap. She shouldn't have asked him a personal question. "Yeah, me too. I mean, I've dated."

"I would have assumed so since you are so beautiful. But, from your tone of voice, it sounds like you had a negative experience dating someone."

"That's part of why I moved here." Olivia appreciated that he thought she was beautiful, which was very nice. But an ache in her chest tightened at the thought of her ex-boyfriend. She didn't miss Geoff; she just hated she had wasted all that time with him and that he had rudely kicked her out of his life.

Marcus surveyed her for a moment before returning to happily eating her food with a look of bliss on his face.

Olivia ate in silence until her curiosity wouldn't stop being curious. "Why did you move to Crawdad Beach?"

He hitched one shoulder. "My sister pressured me and kept telling me what a great place this was and how nice the people were. I found out she was right. It is a great place to live. Plus, I'm enjoying the job."

"It's still just a small town. No nightlife really and not many prospects for us single people." She wasn't looking to go barhopping or anything like that, but Houston had a wide variety of entertainment available.

"I like that there aren't many distractions."

"You don't seem like a guy who gets distracted easily."

"When I'm working, I'm in the zone. It's the after-hours time that can be a problem."

Interesting. Marcus didn't seem like a party-type guy or one who went looking for trouble. "So, what do you do after hours?"

"I work out, then return to work until I need to sleep."

That didn't sound good. "Shouldn't your screen time be limited?" She inwardly cringed. Her question sounded like something her mom would have said. "If you're always inside, how do you stay so tan?"

He gave a soft laugh. "Not much I can do about the screen time. And as for the tanned skin, Mom blessed me with Latin blood. I have a perpetual tan."

"It looks good on you." Why did she say that out loud? Olivia took a bite and chewed.

Marcus tilted his head as his smile brimmed. "Thanks. Nice to hear."

"I'm sure you've heard that before."

His smile dipped. "Yeah, sure. That's what got me in trouble."

"I'm sorry. I shouldn't ask so many questions. It's none of my business." But she still wanted to know.

"It's okay. I've moved on. I have a great job, a nice town with nice people, and one amazing cook I hope will be a good friend."

A rush of heat swelled into her cheeks. "I would like that."

"Good. Now, let me say again, this is one amazing meal."

"You still have dessert waiting."

"Eating your wonderful meals will definitely limit my screen time. I'll need to increase my workout so I don't balloon into a doughy mass."

She chuckled at that thought. "I don't see that happening."

Marcus sighed. "I used to weigh almost three hundred pounds."

She laughed. "You did not!"

"I did." He gave her a wry look. "I was a chunky kid and a fat, geeky teenager."

"No. I don't believe it."

"I have picture proof." His nose scrunched. "Not that I show many people."

Okay, she felt terrible for laughing. "Seriously?"

"Seriously. I started working out in my early twenties, and that's when life got more ... distracting." His eyes held a pained sadness or regret.

"Oh, the women noticed, did they?"

He cleared his throat. "Yes, they did. And I noticed right back, which took me on a downward slide for a few years. I'm very grateful that God was gracious to help me turn things around."

Olivia ignored the God comment. "Thus, the man who now spends all his time working."

He nodded. "It's safer that way. Work during the week, go to church on Sunday, and then work some more."

"Do you think becoming a computer monk is the only way to stay safe?"

Marcus tilted his head as though thinking and then chuckled. "Never heard that one before. Maybe it is. So, are you going to hide in your bakery and become a bakery nun?"

He was teasing, but she wasn't ready to go there. "We aren't talking about me. But I don't know. It's all new."

His right eyebrow elevated. "Oh, so you're just coming off a relationship." His comment didn't sound rude, just curious.

Why was he so perceptive? "Yeah, but it was probably best it ended. He was a jerk. I just ignored that fact along with other of his narcissistic tendencies."

"I'm sorry he hurt you."

Her vision blurred at his kindness. She rose from the table. "I'll go get dessert."

Marcus followed and stood behind her. "I'm sorry for your pain."

She sucked in a breath. Why was he so nice? To keep her hands busy and some level of distance, she took the dessert out of the refrigerator and turned toward Marcus. "I'm over him."

"But not over the heartache." His gentle words rolled over her, tightening her throat.

Olivia squeezed her eyes closed.

His hand rested on her shoulder. "I'm sorry, I shouldn't have said anything."

She pasted on a smile and looked up at his kind eyes. "No, no worries. I shouldn't have gotten so nosy about you." Stepping around him, Olivia set the dessert on the table. She didn't want to talk about Geoff, her anger, or how her heart still hurt. Sure, she had this fantastic opportunity to run her own bakery and not worry about bills, but why couldn't her life be different? Why wasn't her dad here, and why did she waste years dating Geoff?

Olivia served Marcus a slice of dessert, then sat in her chair and put a helping on her plate.

Marcus sat across from her. "I'm sorry about what happened and that the conversation made you uncomfortable. I'll be praying for you to heal."

"Thanks." She didn't mean to sound ungrateful.

His forehead wrinkled, then settled as he turned his attention to his dessert. "This is the best. I can't thank you enough for preparing this for me."

"You're welcome. Baking and cooking makes me happy."

"Your baking and cooking makes me a very happy man."

Once the meal was over, Marcus repeatedly thanked her as he helped her clean the dishes. He limited the conversation to safer topics like the weather and the cute things his nephew said and did.

After they finished, Marcus followed her to the door. "Can I walk you home?"

"No, I'll be fine. It's not exactly far."

Marcus shoved his hands in his jeans pockets. "Again, I'm sorry I brought up a painful subject for you. I'll try to do better next time. That is if you still want to continue. I'll understand if it's too much with all you have going on with preparing for your bakery to open."

Olivia stared at the hardwood floors beneath her feet. She probably shouldn't cook his meals and come to his apartment, but something behind his kind eyes drew her toward him. "No, I'm fine. I'd like to keep doing this for you."

"I really appreciate it, Olivia. I like being around you. No strings attached, okay?"

Even though she nodded, part of her felt a little disappointed. She wouldn't mind being at least a tiny bit attached to Marcus.

They said a final goodbye, and Olivia walked back to her apartment and sat on her couch. Why did she ruin the evening by getting all moody? Why couldn't she let the past go and enjoy the new things? Why couldn't she think more positively?

She wanted the peace she'd seen on Marcus's face when he talked about God. She wanted the peace that her mom, Jennifer, her grandad, and most of her family had that she couldn't grasp.

Olivia shoved a hair behind her ear. She missed the peace she'd felt when she was younger before her dad died. Why had God abandoned her?

I'm still here.

The gentle words flowed through her mind, wrapping around her heart.

Was that her thought, or would God be kind enough to reach out to her? Her mom and grandad would tell her that God loves her and wanted her to trust Him and return to Him.

Olivia kicked off her shoes and stomped to her bedroom. Maybe it was true that God loved her and wanted her to trust Him, but could she trust God?

Chapter 5

Groggy from lack of sleep, Olivia held her computer tablet as she inventoried her storage room supplies. Based on her calculations, she had everything needed to open the bakery. Since her cousin David was the local grocery store manager, and his family owned the business, he gave her a fantastic deal on the essentials of flour, sugar, eggs, butter, spices, and almost every item needed for the bakery.

She had tossed and turned last night, thinking about all the time she'd wasted dating Geoff, along with her many mistakes. If God hadn't taken her dad, maybe things would have been different. Olivia sighed. She still couldn't believe her grandad's generosity and that even her mom had chipped in from her savings for operating expenses.

Crawdad Beach already felt like home since everyone was so nice to her. She sure didn't deserve their kindness.

"You need to just go for it." Grinning, her mom leaned against the open door jamb. "Please stop waiting on me to open the bakery. I don't know when I'll have my next surgery, and you need to enjoy this wonderful gift you've been given." Her beautiful mom looked so happy since she married Eric, the owner of Doohickeys hardware store. They had grown up in Crawdad Beach and dated in high school. Since they were both widowed, they reconnected once Olivia and her mom moved to town. Olivia was happy for them, but it was strange that, at twenty-three, she had a stepdad. Fortunately, she really liked Eric, and Crystal seemed blissfully happy. After seven years of being a widow, her mom did deserve happiness.

As for the bakery? Her mom was right. It was time. Olivia needed to get customers in the door and start paying back her grandad and mom. No one expected Olivia to do that, but she wanted to prove to them and herself that she could be a success.

Olivia took a deep breath and glanced at her mom. "Okay, I'll think about it. When I open, I'll probably choose a Monday. That way, I might not be as busy as a weekend, so we can take care of anything that might go wrong."

"Everything will go great. You've been baking for weeks and having taste testings with family and friends. Everyone adores your pastries. It's time to share your goodies with the rest of the world."

Olivia saved her work on her computer tablet. "Ha, the rest of the world would be nice, but that would mean a whole lot of work." She stepped closer to her mom. "But before I do anything, I want to make sure you're okay."

"I'm fine." Her mom waved a dismissive hand. "I'm

still a little sore from the surgery, so I'm in no hurry to fix the other areas. I want to enjoy my new husband and help you."

Olivia sent her a mock glare. "You two are rather disgusting with all your kissy-face stuff."

Grinning, her mom's eyes got that far-away dreamy look. "He is a good kisser."

Olivia held up her hand. "Please, no details."

Her mom's expression turned serious. "You do know no one will replace your father. Sean was a wonderful husband and dad."

"Yeah, he was." Olivia inwardly groaned. "I still miss him."

"We were blessed to have the years we did with Sean."

"I hate cancer," Olivia growled. After all these years, why couldn't someone develop a cure?

"Me too, honey. Me, too. Eric is my new husband, but no one will replace your dad."

"I know that. It's been years since Dad died, and I'm not a little kid anymore."

"You don't need to wait to open. Please let me help. You are a wonderful baker, and this town and all those who come to visit need to taste your amazing creations."

Olivia bit her lip. She was right. It was time. "Okay, I'll do it. Next Monday will be the grand opening."

Her mom did a happy dance, or at least as much as

she could with her limp. The poor woman had no coordination whatsoever.

Olivia cringed. "Please, no dancing. It was bad enough before you had your surgery. Now you look even more lopsided. We were hoping the surgeon would implant some coordination in you."

Her mom grinned. "Well, Eric likes my dancing."

"I'm sure he does. You two make a great pair since he also has no rhythm. Good thing we didn't have a dance at your wedding."

"We did miss that opportunity, didn't we?" Her mom gave her a mischievous look that said trouble was brewing. "Maybe we could dance for your grand opening?"

"Oh, no, mother. Please, no. I do *not* want nauseous customers."

"Alright, I'll behave myself. And you need to get your skinny, little tail in gear and open your bakery."

Olivia grinned as she gave her mom a side-eye glance. "Yes, mother."

They walked toward the kitchen, and Olivia paused to admire the mural her cousin had painted on the wall of a cute cartoon crawdad wearing a teal apron and holding a rolling pin in one of his claws and an oven mitt in the other.

Her mom stood next to her. "I love what you had Tess draw. It's so cute. Olivia, everything in here is just perfect.

The little bistro tables, the old bike that Jeremy refinished for you and hung on the wall, the display cabinet of antique bakery tools on the other wall, and the cute teal and white awning out front will welcome customers into your beautiful bakery."

"Everything does look great. I am excited to get going." Olivia walked to the kitchen to see if her dough had risen.

Her mom followed and leaned against the stainless steel prep table. "I heard an interesting rumor that you're cooking meals for a handsome bachelor."

"Small-town news sure does travel fast."

"I've heard he's a sweet young man."

"You sure do hear a lot." Olivia placed the dough on the work surface and took her rolling pin in hand. "Marcus is probably too sweet for me." She flattened and prepared the dough for the next steps.

"What? Why would you say such a thing? You are a sweet, precious young woman."

"You're my mom. You're supposed to say stuff like that."

"I don't think it's in the mom handbook. I love you, and that will never change."

Olivia didn't comment. If she truly knew everything Olivia had done, her mom probably wouldn't feel that way.

The morning passed quickly as Jennifer and her mom helped with baking. Olivia's cousin Tess made graphics to place on Rolling in the Dough's website and social media pages, and then she made flyers to put up around town.

After everyone left for the day, Olivia rushed upstairs to her apartment to prepare a meal for Marcus. Since he'd mentioned he had a weight problem when he was younger, she was determined to find a healthy dish to make his tastebuds happy. She had difficulty picturing him overweight because he was *very* in shape now.

Did he have a girlfriend? If not, why not? He should have women lined up at his door. Did he spend so much time on his computer that he didn't have time to date anyone? If that was true, she had an opportunity to spend time with him that other women didn't.

What was she thinking? Why would he be interested in her? He obviously had a relationship with God, which meant he wouldn't want anything to do with her.

When her dad died, her church friends had at first been supportive. However, as her anger at God grew, she pulled away from her church youth group and started hanging out with those considered the "bad" kids. Most of her church friends turned their back on her.

With church people and with God, she was no longer welcome.

Since Marcus had set the alarm for five o'clock, he had time to finish his day's work, grab a quick shower, and set the table before Olivia arrived. At five-thirty-two, she knocked.

Marcus opened the door, and she stood there wearing jeans and a cute sweater top.

She held up an insulated delivery bag. "Dinner is served."

He tried not to drool. "I have been looking forward to seeing you all day." He didn't bother to clarify what he meant.

"Well, thank you. It's good to see you too. But I bet you say that to all the food delivery people."

"Nope. You are the first."

Her cheeks reddened. Turning away, she walked to the table and took out the dishes she'd brought. "For your dining pleasure, I have Herbed Chicken Marsala, broccoli, and angel food cake with strawberries and blueberries."

"Sounds yummy and healthy. Is this because you found out I had been overweight?"

"Well... Yes, I'm sorry." Her forehead wrinkled.

"No, don't apologize. The meal looks and smells wonderful. If it's healthy, that's even better."

"You don't mind?"

"Of course not. Thank you. What you did is very thoughtful. Will you join me this evening?" Marcus pulled out a chair for her.

Olivia lifted a shoulder. "You don't need me to stay."

"It would be an honor to be blessed with your company."

"Well, how could I refuse when you say it like that?"

He waited until she settled before he sat across from her and held his hand out toward her. "Mind if I pray?"

Olivia gave him a tentative nod and put her hand in his.

He prayed and thanked God for the meal, for God's many blessings, and for Olivia. Marcus kept the prayer honest and sincere, but he didn't go into the many prayers he had prayed for Olivia through the night. When he finished, he squeezed her fingers and released her soft hand.

Tears shimmered in her eyes as she lifted her head.

He leaned toward her. "Are you okay?"

"Oh, yes. I'm fine." Her words didn't match her expression. "I just didn't sleep very well last night."

"I'm sorry." Was cooking his meal a problem for her?

Olivia looked like she would say something but instead dished out a helping for his plate. "I hope you like the food."

"I'm sure I will. I can't thank you enough for doing this for me. And, Olivia, remember, if this is too much for you, please don't hesitate to let me know."

"No, I enjoy cooking something other than pastries.

And I wouldn't eat like this if I was cooking just for myself."

Marcus took a bite and chewed. "This is so good. Your meals are better than I've had in the finest restaurants in Los Angeles."

Olivia's head snapped up. "You lived there?"

He mentally slapped himself on the head for sharing that fact. "Yeah, for a few years."

"Did you like it?"

"It was okay. California weather can be nice, but there are too many people, too many cars, too much going on, and it is very expensive." He would not share the rest with her or anyone else.

"Was Crawdad Beach a shock?"

"Yes," he chuckled, "but a good one. I love the small-town atmosphere, and the people are amazing. I'm glad I'm here. How about you?"

"I'm happy to be here too. I wish I had been here sooner, though. Maybe things would be different." Vulnerability flashed in her eyes.

"We can't change the past."

"I wish we could." Her voice was only a whisper.

He understood that statement. If only he could write computer code to remove a few of his past years. Man, he'd be a gazillionaire if he could write a software package to do that for the general public.

What did Olivia want to change? She came from a

great family. Her grandad, Henry Doss, was a Godly man. Marcus had even met most of Olivia's family at church or around town.

They continue to eat in silence. Once Marcus finished, he put down his fork. "So, do you have a date for opening your bakery?"

"I actually do. Next Monday will be the grand opening."

"That's great. I can't wait to try everything you have on the menu."

Olivia cut the angel food cake she'd brought, slid a helping on his plate, and topped it with a mixture of blueberries and strawberries. "If you do, you might not be able to fit out of the door."

"I didn't mean I'd eat everything all at once. However, I did have a buddy in college who went to a restaurant and ordered everything on the menu. And he ate it all."

She gasped. "No. Please tell me the guy shared with other people or was a giant or something."

"He was big. Played lineman for our university and pretty much took up the whole line. He worked out in the gym when he wasn't in class or on the football field. I've never seen anyone lift weights as much as he did. He was massive." Marcus took a bite of the delicious dessert and tried not to moan again.

"I can't imagine. I don't work out." She took a dainty bite of food.

"You stay in great shape." Not that he had noticed a time or two or three or four.

"Thanks." She averted her gaze. "I guess I get cardio from running around in the kitchen. I pretty much stay on my feet all day."

"You must be exhausted. I sit in front of computer screens all day. Man, it makes me feel bad that you're spending extra time in the kitchen cooking for me."

"No, really, I enjoy baking and cooking. It's my happy place."

"Still, I want you to tell me if you want to stop or take off a few days. Okay?"

"Okay. I promise."

Heat crawled up his neck as he admired her big brown eyes. He could get in trouble with Olivia very fast if he didn't stay focused.

Once they finished eating, he helped her clean and pack her dishes. She took a seat on the couch, and he sat across from her in his chair. With a pretty woman who could cook like a five-star chef, he needed to keep a safe distance.

Their conversation flowed when he asked questions about the bakery, but he noticed that Olivia would either avoid answering or change the subject away from personal questions. Of course, he did the same. There were some things in his past that he didn't ever want to become public knowledge.

He walked her back to her place and, in an awkward goodbye, gave her a quick hug. He'd have preferred something more intimate, but he needed to keep away from a temptation situation. Olivia was right about something she mentioned in an earlier conversation; he had become a computer monk.

Safely back in his apartment, he went to his office and checked his messages.

Marcus's stomach rolled as he stared at the cryptic message on his computer monitor. He shook his head. *No, it must be a sick joke.* He'd covered his tracks. How did they know what he did and where to find him?

Fifteen years ago, he'd been a cocky teenage hacker who thought he was just having fun. But fun and games ended when he hacked the wrong website. After all these years, they'd tracked him down.

And they expected him to pay.

Chapter 6

Five dozen cupcakes and six-layer cakes of various flavors were now in the bakery freezer. Olivia preferred and planned on making fresh products every morning, but she wanted to be ready for whatever happened once the doors opened for business.

After saying goodbye to Jennifer, Olivia hurried upstairs to prepare a meal for Marcus. Thank goodness her family members owned and managed the local grocery store. No matter what she needed, they were happy to take orders for the bakery or for her personal use.

Even though she was tired after being on her feet all day, the thought of spending an evening with Marcus boosted her energy. She would enjoy his company without over-enjoying his company. It was okay to be attracted to Marcus, but she needed to protect her heart. The wounds Geoff had inflicted still were sore and raw. He had used her for years, and she had been so out of touch with reality that she hadn't even noticed until it was too late.

Olivia cooked the meal for Marcus. She quickly showered while everything stayed warm on the stove and oven. Once finished, she placed the dishes in her delivery bag and hurried to his apartment.

She knocked and waited. And waited. She knocked louder.

The door opened. Marcus stared at her like he didn't even know who she was. Dark circles lined his eyes, and his hair was a mess. He looked like he hadn't slept in a week.

Olivia held up her bag. "Did you forget I was bringing dinner?"

He took off his glasses and rubbed his eyes. "Is it dinner time?"

"It's five thirty in the evening."

"Oh." He stepped aside and motioned for her to enter.

"Have you eaten since yesterday?"

Marcus shrugged. "I don't think so." He closed the door behind her, followed her to his table, and sank into a chair.

"Are you feeling okay?"

He put his head in his hands. "I'm not sick."

She set down the bag and went to the kitchen to get plates and silverware. "Want to tell me what's wrong?" Not that was her business, but she was curious.

"No. It's not you. It's something personal I need to work on."

"Do you feel like eating? I made chicken fajitas with sautéed peppers and onions, homemade flour tortillas,

Pico de Gallo, sour cream, mixed cheeses, Mexican garlic butter, Mexican Rice & charro beans, and guacamole, chips, and homemade salsa."

His head jerked up. "You would do that for me?"

"Of course." He looked like a lost little boy; she wanted to put her arms around him and tell him it would be okay. "I'm sorry for whatever is going on."

"Thanks." He averted his gaze for a moment. "And thank you for dinner. Will you stay with me, please? I could use a friend."

Her heart thumped against her chest wall as though telling her she didn't need to worry about protecting herself. Marcus needed her help. "Just stay here, and I'll get everything out for you." She arranged the dishes on the table and sat across from him.

He put his head back in his hands.

What happened to make him so troubled? Several unpleasant ideas ran through her mind. Was he having old girlfriend problems? Family problems? Business problems? Olivia sat and waited. Would Marcus pray, or should she just eat or put everything on his plate for him?

Marcus raised his head. "I'm sorry. I should pray." He offered his hand and waited for her to place her hand in his. Bowing his head, he sat still. "Oh, God..."

Olivia squeezed his fingers. Did a family member die? Not knowing what else to do, she sent up a silent prayer for help for Marcus. Maybe God would listen to her prayers since she was praying for someone else.

Marcus groaned and released her fingers. "Sorry about that. It's just been a rough twenty-four hours. I'm battling a bad cyber-attack. Plus, lack of sleep and hunger must have gotten to me. Your food smells amazing, and I need to eat."

"Don't let me stop you."

He loaded his plate and ate like he hadn't seen food in a week. "This is so good. So good. Thank you."

"I'm glad you like it because chicken fajitas are one of my favorite foods. My mom makes an amazing homemade salsa."

Marcus scooped a chip in the salsa, chewed, and swallowed. "Wow, that's great. Thank you. I'm feeling better already."

"Mom says salsa makes everything better."

His eyes still looked sad, but he grinned. "Crystal is a wise woman. I'm starting to feel human again."

She let Marcus eat in peace. Until she realized she'd forgotten to make a dessert. Bummer. "I'm so sorry. I forgot to bring dessert."

He looked at her and blinked. "Really? A baker forgot dessert?" His grin looked more like himself.

"Don't tell anyone."

"Your secret is safe with me."

When they finished the meal, she left him the leftovers.

Marcus helped her pack up her remaining dishes. "I'd love to have you stay, but I need to get back to work."

"Is there anything I can help you with?"

"I wish there were." He walked her to the door and took her in his arms. "Thank you for coming over."

She felt so good against his muscular chest.

He kissed the top of her head and released her. "See you tomorrow?"

"I'll be here around five-thirty. Call me if I can do anything, okay?" At his nod, she said goodbye.

The door shut and locked behind her. What on earth had happened to Marcus?

Olivia made her way down the stairs. Why had he been so sad? He said he wasn't sick that it was something about a cyber-attack. But that was his business. Why would something like that matter?

Maybe, like her, Marcus had secrets he didn't want to share with anyone.

Staring blankly at the computer screen, Marcus sat at his desk. His past attacking him had been completely unexpected. Repercussions after fifteen years, seemed crazy, and he hadn't been able to pull himself together. He should have showered, eaten something, and at least gotten a few hours of sleep instead of sending his body and emotions into a tailspin.

Marcus shoved out of his seat and hit the floor. He needed to do a hundred pushups or five hundred to get out his frustration. He made it to fifty before collapsing.

Rolling over, he stared at the ceiling. Since receiving that cryptic message, he'd been hit with another cyber-attack that kept him up all night. He'd successfully stopped them from taking down his system, but he knew they would try again.

Marcus contacted the cyber-defense community for ideas, asking his ethical hacker friends for help. But more importantly, Marcus had prayed and prayed and prayed.

He'd spent his career being the good guy to try and make up for what he'd done when he was fifteen. He'd been the one who came to rescue those who had been hit by evil hackers. Now, he was the one under attack and smart enough to know if he paid them, they would not stop.

His cell phone signaled an incoming text. One of his cyber-buddies had an idea. Marcus placed the call to his friend.

Chapter 7

Feeling like he had been hit in the head by a boulder, Marcus disconnected the call. All this time, he thought his cyber-buddy, Dragon-Slayer58, was a guy.

They'd been online friends for years and worked together on many cybersecurity projects but never talked on the phone before today. Over the years Marcus had reached out for help in personal matters. Although he'd always received great advice, he thought he was discussing things with another man.

Groaning, Marcus shook his head trying to clear his thoughts. His world had tilted on its axis. To top off his confusion, the woman sounded older. How could that be true?

Talking about women problems to an older woman made him cringe. Even though sometimes he went to his mom for advice, he would never, *ever* have gone into the detail he'd gone into when he thought he was sharing with another guy.

Marcus shuddered. The woman must think him an absolute reprobate because when he was in Los Angeles attending parties and dating women he shouldn't have been dating, Dragon-Slayer58 had been his sounding board helping him get on the right track with God.

He had known his friend was a Christian but never thought it was an older woman. She had been delighted to hear his voice. But, him? Not so much. What if fifty-eight was her birth year?

Oh. My. Goodness. She would be older than his grandmother!

What had he done? He'd even shared about his attraction with Olivia.

Marcus got up and paced in his office. What was he supposed to do now? The friendship hadn't bothered her, but how could he go on knowing his dragon buddy was a dragon lady? The visuals that came to mind were not pretty.

Whoever the woman was, she had helped him take out hackers and helped him with his problems, but it still felt weird and awkward that he had been sharing so many things with her.

Whatever he decided about their friendship, she gave him great advice about his current problem. He just hoped it worked.

Olivia and Jennifer spent the day baking, tweaking recipes, making sure they had notes on what needed to be done each day, and deciding what specials they would run. Olivia probably should have waited to hire Jennifer once she opened, but she didn't want to rely solely on her family to help. Plus, Jennifer turned out to be more than an employee; she was a great friend.

Checking the accounting software, Olivia sighed. She desperately needed to start making money. The outflow kept flowing, but there was no inflow. In just a few more days, she'd open the bakery, and hopefully, it would be profitable.

The bell over the front door dinged, signaling someone's arrival. Olivia peeked out of the office and grinned.

Her grandad and his friend, Chester, walked toward her.

"Got any afternoon yummies ready for us?" Chester asked as he patted his flat stomach.

"Sure do." Olivia motioned for them to follow her to the kitchen.

"Hi, Mr. Chester and Mr. Henry." Jennifer smiled at the men. "Y'all ready to try what we baked?"

"You betcha!" Chester pointed to a chocolate cupcake.

"This is our favorite time of the day now," her grandad said. "Once you open, it will be hard not to visit every few hours. May I try the white cupcake with sprinkles, please?"

"Henry," Chester said, "we might have to do more than fish in the mornings. Should we take up walking or something so we don't turn into roly-polies? We better exercise to keep our amazing physiques." He struck a body-builder pose.

Olivia grinned at Chester and then handed them both napkins with the cupcakes. "Come any time the doors are open. I don't think either of you will have any problems staying in shape. You're both always in motion doing something around town."

"True," Chester said. "We do stay pretty busy helping Jeremy in his workshop for Knick Knacks and doing other things."

"And you and Maybelline travel several days a week to pick up products for Jeremy," Her grandad added.

"Yeah, and you stay busy helping your family or babysitting your great-grandkids." Chester bit into the cupcake and sighed. "Yum. Hey, what else did you put in this? It's got kind of a kick. A really good kick."

Olivia grinned at his surprised reaction. "We put a touch of cinnamon and cayenne in the chocolate."

"Oh, man. These are great." Chester devoured the treat in a few bites.

Her grandad took a bite of his, chewed, and wiped his face. "Excellent, ladies." He chewed slowly while contentedly smiling.

Chester's gaze rested on a sheet of cookies. "Are

those for sampling too?"

Jennifer handed him one still warm from the oven. "With Thanksgiving coming next month, this is our raisin spice cookie."

Chester took a big bite. "Wow. It dances a happy dance on my tongue."

Olivia grinned. If customers liked the baked goods as much as Chester and Granddad did, she would truly be rolling in the dough.

"So, missy, are you still cooking for Marcus?" Chester's mischievous grin made Olivia's face flame with heat.

"Yes, I'm still cooking for him." She grinned back at Chester, then busied herself with placing the cookies on a decorative plate.

"Is that keeping you too busy?" Her grandad eyed her with a worried look.

"So far, it's been fine. If it becomes too much, I'll step away. Don't worry, I'm doing what I love. And cooking for Marcus in the evenings also gives me a great meal to eat.

"Good girl. I want you to take care of yourself."

The door chimed, and her mom and Eric came in, followed by the rest of her family.

Her mom handed Olivia a stack of disposable plates and brown paper sacks. "I figured you could use these for the hungry horde." She grinned as she motioned toward the rest of the family.

Eric handed Olivia a large glass jar filled with money. "You can set this on the counter for tips. The family chipped in to get you started."

Olivia stared wide-eyed at the overflowing container with everything from coins to hundred-dollar bills. "Oh, my goodness. I can't believe it. Thank you all." She blinked through the moisture building in her eyes. "You are all so sweet to me. Thank you."

"You're the sweet one." Chester held up another cupcake. "Besides that, we figured we had probably eaten several hundred dollars of your inventory."

Olivia's mom hugged her. "We wanted you to know how much we appreciate you sharing your wonderful talent with us."

Chester motioned with his hands. "For she's a jolly good woman." He sang out, and the rest joined him in a rousing, slightly off-key song. "For she's a jolly good woman. For she's a jolly good woman, which nobody can deny!"

"Please don't forget Jennifer," Olivia wiped happy tears away and turned to her friend.

The group sang another round of the song, followed by cheers and applause.

Olivia felt like her smile would break her face open as her family and friends helped themselves to the bakery items they had prepared.

After everyone left, she and Jennifer cleaned the

kitchen and counted the money in the tip jar. Olivia couldn't believe it. Her friends and family had given her $753.48. Olivia gave half to Jennifer.

Her friend gasped and held up her hands. "No, the money was for you and your bakery."

"It's for you, too. You've been helping. Please take it."

Jennifer's hand shook. "Really? Thank you. You don't know how much this means to me. My husband and I had a bill come due the other day, and we prayed and asked God for help, and look what He did!" She looked up at the ceiling. "Thank you, Jesus!"

Olivia chuckled as her friend danced a little jig.

Jennifer hung up her apron and grabbed her purse. "I can't wait to get home and tell my husband. I mean, if you're okay with me leaving right now."

"Yes, go home and enjoy your evening." Olivia giggled as her friend squealed and ran out the door.

After finishing cleaning up, Olivia went upstairs to cook Marcus a meal. She sure hoped he would be in a better disposition tonight and maybe tell her what upset him.

Either way, she had steak, baked potatoes, and salad for his dinner and molten chocolate cupcakes for dessert. The dinner wouldn't be low-calorie, but hopefully, it would brighten his mood.

Chapter 8

It worked!

Marcus pumped a fist in the air. After hours of analyzing and digging deep, he'd finally traced the original domain and IP address behind the cryptic message and cyber-attack. The culprit had used a self-erasing code and routed their IP through multiple countries.

With Dragon-Slayer58's help, they had taken down the evil person or persons. Since the hackers were with a foreign entity that also had been attacking the United States, Marcus reported their findings to the government. The hackers wouldn't bother him or anyone else for a long time. Marcus thanked God and sent a thank you message to his friend.

As much as he appreciated his friend's help, he was still freaked out that she was a woman. He planned to stay in touch and visit her online; he just wouldn't be as free to mention his dating problems.

Marcus checked the time. He had three hours to complete the assignment for his regular job, shower, and be ready when Olivia stopped by this evening.

Hopefully, she didn't think him strange or weird

because of his reaction the last time she was here. He had acted like his world was ending. Maybe because part of him had thought that would happen, that his past sins would be broadcast to the world. He knew God had forgiven him, but accepting God's forgiveness could often be challenging.

As for the hackers? They might have been stopped this time, but the chances and severity of another attack were now elevated. The attackers would be livid that they had been stopped. Marcus squeezed his eyes shut. He couldn't let down his guard for a moment because he might have just started a firestorm.

His door opened before Olivia even knocked.

Clean-shaven and smelling nice, Marcus grinned as he held the door open for her to come inside. "I've been looking forward to seeing you all day."

"It's good to see you too." She walked to his already set table, put down her bag, and removed the covered dishes.

"Thanks again for coming over. So, what did you bring?"

"Since you seemed to have such a rough day yesterday, I brought steak, baked potatoes, salad, and molten chocolate cupcakes for dessert."

"Oh, man. You are the best." He pulled out her chair and waited until she sat.

He settled across from her and reached his hand toward her. "I'll pray and bless the food."

Marcus prayed in a respectful way, yet as if he were talking to someone close and familiar. Her granddad prayed like that, sweet prayers that made her feel like he had taken her with him into God's throne room. Why couldn't her prayers be like that?

Prayer over, Marcus squeezed her fingers and released her hand.

She smiled at him. "You are in a better mood than yesterday."

"That's an understatement. The worst-case scenario I envisioned did not happen."

"The world didn't implode?"

"Nope. A friend helped me take care of the situation. Actually, God should get all the credit." He helped himself to a healthy portion and ate with his usual moans of pleasure.

She enjoyed the meal with him until her curiosity got the better of her. "You seemed really worried yesterday."

"I *was* worried." Marcus set down his fork. "I should have explained things yesterday, but honestly, I was embarrassed."

"Well, I had imagined all sorts of interesting scenarios about you being upset. Old girlfriends, death of a family or friend, or you had lost your job or something like that."

He sighed and sat back in his chair. "I was dealing with something I did when I was fifteen." He looked away for a moment. "I had hacked a website. I didn't mean anything by it and thought I was just having harmless fun. The problem was that the website was not a nice one, and the people who ran it did not find my hacking humorous. Yesterday, they tracked me down."

Olivia gasped. "After all these years? And why are you telling me this if you're embarrassed about what you did?"

One of his shoulders raised. "A friend reminded me that what we hide in the dark doesn't go away; it just gets darker. We have to bring it to God's light and be honest with Him about what we've done. And sometimes we share our failures with others so that they will learn from our mistakes and know that God is patient, kind, and forgiving."

She took a bite of her food and chewed, trying to think of a response about God's forgiveness. She wasn't ready to agree with him on that subject. Instead, she kept the conversation focused on Marcus. "How did the bad guys find you and know it was you? What did they want?"

"I'm not sure how they found me, but they did want me to pay."

Imagining all kinds of terrible repercussions, Olivia cringed. "How? Are they going to break your legs or something?"

"No, they wanted money. Lots of money." Marcus ran his hand through his hair. "Fortunately, God was gracious to help me figure out what to do through an ethical hacker friend."

"Ethical hackers? I didn't know something like that existed. I thought all hackers were bad."

"Ethical hackers work within the confines of the law. A person or an organization employs them, and they follow a strict code of ethics to ensure their actions help rather than harm. They assist companies or website owners in improving their network defenses."

"Is that what you do?"

He nodded. "I'm employed as a cybersecurity specialist by Dustin Bowman's firm here in town, and I also moonlight as an ethical hacker."

"So, you're one of the good guys?"

"I try to be, hope to be, and pray to be."

Olivia cocked an eyebrow. "That's a lot for one person to be."

"To be or not to be is *not* the question. I want to be pleasing to God in what I do and say." Marcus cut a bite off his steak and grinned her way. "I've got a long way to go, but I'm trying."

Olivia tried to give him a pleasant smile. Since moving to Crawdad Beach, her life had changed in a positive way. Maybe that would be pleasing to God? Even though she was trying to live better, she'd made too many mistakes.

Marcus wiped his mouth. "You asked me once if my friends were in person or online. I do have friends who I meet with in person." He squirmed in his chair as differing expressions crossed his face as though trying to decide what to share with her. "One of my online ethical hacker friends has extraordinary talent. I've messaged with that person for years as we took down evil hackers. I had freely shared my personal struggles, thinking Dragon-Slayer58 was a cyber-buddy about my age, but I learned yesterday that the person is actually a woman born in 1958."

"No! Are you kidding me?"

"No, I am not. I am embarrassed to say that over the years, I bared my heart to a woman older than my grandmother."

Olivia snorted a laugh. "Oh, that is too funny." Embarrassed at her unladylike outburst, she covered her mouth but couldn't stop laughing.

He laughed with her. "So, having a real, in-the-flesh friend is pretty special—especially a beautiful friend who is an amazing chef."

Heat rose from her toes to the top of her head as she stared into his eyes. "I'll get the dessert." She got to her feet.

"Isn't it right here?" Marcus pointed to the open delivery bag.

"Right. I mean, I'll get us dessert plates." Olivia

retreated to his kitchen and opened a cabinet door. Her face had to be glowing red. This wasn't the first time Marcus said she was beautiful. Why was he so nice to her?

Geoff had only complimented her looks when he wanted something from her. And that something was not pleasing to God.

Maybe Marcus was being friendly so she would have a physical relationship with him? No, she didn't need to think like that. Marcus hadn't done anything that led her to believe he wanted anything more than friendship. Could that even happen? Could she just be a friend with him? If he were trying to live pleasing to God, he should be on his best behavior. Interesting. The bigger question was, could she behave?

Olivia grabbed two plates and went back to the table.

"I was worried you got lost," Marcus grinned.

"No, I was just thinking."

"I'm sorry if my comment made you uncomfortable."

"Uncomfortable? No. Complimenting the chef is a smart move."

"Ah, well, that won't be a problem. Your cooking is worthy of compliments. And you are very lovely." His smile made heat flash up her back.

She playfully narrowed her eyes. "Two can play this game, you know."

His eyebrows rose. "Really? Is that a promise or a threat?"

"Both. My very handsome cybersecurity, ethical hacker friend."

His eyes widened for a moment, and his neck reddened. Well, look at that. Marcus could be embarrassed. Oh, now she could have fun. But could she have fun without getting them both in trouble?

Chapter 9

Another sleepless night. Marcus groggily ate a protein bar as he sat at his desk. The evening with Olivia had gone far too well. She was a gorgeous first-class chef and baker, and her sense of humor had come out full force, making her a deadly combination. He could get in trouble way too fast. Other than what seemed to be her lack of faith, she was the perfect woman.

Not only did he need to be on guard for another cyber-attack, he needed to keep himself out of trouble with Olivia. In the past, Marcus would reach out to Dragon-Slayer for advice and prayer.

Now, what was he supposed to do? He had other friends he could call, text, or email, but he'd lost who he thought was his best buddy.

Marcus groaned. Why had he hired Olivia to cook for him? Why did he brag that he wanted to live a life pleasing to God? It was true, but it was easier when he stayed isolated.

What was that verse about temptation? Marcus opened the online Bible app to read the Amplified version of First Corinthians 10:13. The verse promised that regardless of the source of temptation, our compassionate, trustworthy God would not let us be tempted beyond our ability, providing us help to endure and overcome. Marcus printed the verse to keep in front of him. He needed his faithful God to help him be faithful.

Last night, when he was praying, he didn't sense that he needed to step away from Olivia, but he did need to be careful. Being alone with her in his apartment wouldn't make things easy.

Marcus sighed. He could stop cyber-attacks. He just wasn't sure how well he would resist a temptation attack.

Olivia had barely slept last night from thinking about Marcus, but she still felt energized. Teasing Marcus had been fun, and she planned on doing much more of that. Humming a tune, she poured the batter into a cake pan and popped it in the oven.

"You sure are in a good mood this morning." Jennifer grinned at her.

"I had a nice evening, and today is the last weekday before we open on Monday."

"Are you excited?"

It took a moment for Olivia to reign in her Marcus thoughts. "Yes, I'm super excited about opening the bakery. I can't believe it's almost here." Olivia poured a cup of coffee for each of them. "What do you think about this blend?"

Jennifer took a sip. "That's good."

"I know, right? David ordered it for us."

"You are blessed to have family who own the local grocery store. God's fingerprints are all over you, coming here and getting your own building and bakery. It's amazing and fun to be a part of your journey."

Olivia blinked. *God's fingerprints?* Was that true? She couldn't deny what had happened to her since she'd moved to Crawdad Beach. She would never have thought she'd have a building with a great apartment and a bakery she'd designed, all debt-free by her grandad.

Were those blessings really God-given? She sure didn't deserve anything since she'd pushed God away.

Her phone signaled a text message. She pulled her phone from her jeans pocket and grinned. Marcus asked that instead of cooking for him this evening, she would join him after work for dinner and then for a walk on the beach. Dinner was his treat.

Sounded good to her. She sent Marcus a quick yes. Now, what should she wear? She checked her phone's weather app. Since it was mid-October, the temperature in South Carolina was still reasonably warm, but it was not her idea of swimming weather. She could wear shorts, but what if he meant he was taking her to a nice restaurant? Olivia typed back a question. *Are we eating out or eating on the beach?*

He returned a happy face emoji and told her to dress nice enough to eat at a restaurant but casual enough to walk on the beach. He would pick her up in his car when she let him know she was finished for the day.

Olivia sent him a thumbs-up and then a smiling face emoji. Thank goodness she had a casual but classy dress. Dining with Marcus and then strolling beside him on a beach sounded very nice.

"Everything okay?" Jennifer asked.

"Yes, everything is great."

Jennifer chuckled. "By the dreamy look on your face, I imagine the texts were from Marcus?"

"You would imagine correctly. He's taking me to dinner, and then we'll walk on the beach."

"How nice. Sounds serious."

Olivia shook her head. "No, we're just friends." Not that she wouldn't mind more than a friendship, but he wouldn't want that. Not with someone like her. "Back to work. I'd like us to finish baking five more cakes to freeze and have them ready to display when we open on Monday."

Jennifer nodded. "I'm making two round cakes to decorate. One for a boy's birthday and the other for a girl's birthday."

"Good. I'll prepare a small two-tier wedding cake, and we can make several sheet cakes and come up with some fun ideas for decorating them. Having these ready will give our customers ideas on what we can do for them. Monday morning, and every morning after that, we'll bake new items to serve fresh and hot."

Olivia watched the time as they continued working. Thankfully, they were through baking, cleaning, and letting the cakes rest before setting them in the freezer by three-thirty.

Once they finished, she sent Jennifer home. Olivia wanted to shower and prepare for her evening with Marcus. Not that it was a date or anything. Or was it a date? Her heart fluttered at that thought. Whatever the evening held, she wanted to be ready.

Once Olivia was clean and dressed, she sent Marcus a text. He replied that he would leave and be in front of her building in a few minutes. He would be driving a dark blue SUV.

She checked herself in the mirror and went downstairs to wait by the front door. Along Main Street's sidewalk, a young woman pushed a stroller, an older couple walked their little white dog, and her mom and Eric walked hand in hand as they entered Tiddlywinks restaurant.

Marcus parked and hurried toward her as she stepped out of the building. "Ready to go?"

"I guess so." She closed and locked the door behind her before turning to him. "Is what I'm wearing okay?"

"You look very nice." His smile heated her cheeks.

Marcus opened the SUV door for her, waited until she buckled in, and then hurried to his side. He slid in his seat, started the car, and drove slowly through town. "I hope you're hungry. Chester told me about a great seafood place."

"Chester? You do know that could make things interesting."

"True." With a panicked look, Marcus swung his gaze toward her. "He does have a quirky sense of humor. Hopefully, it will be okay." Marcus didn't sound so sure.

"If Chester said it was good, it will be good."

"Well, we'll take our chances. Thanks for letting me take you out. I love your cooking, but I figured maybe you needed a break with everything you have going on."

"I appreciate this. It's been a while since I've been on a date." She stopped herself. "I mean. I know this isn't a date; I meant going out with a guy. I mean. Oh, I don't know what I mean." Geoff never took her out since he was the restaurant chef where they both worked. Eating out wasn't something they did. Come to think of it, why didn't he ever take her out? They never did anything together other than work and then go to his place. Ugh. Why did she waste years dating him?

Marcus slid his gaze her way. "Let's just say we are friends checking out a new restaurant together."

"Okay, I'll go with that." Olivia smiled at him, but part

of her was a little disappointed. She wouldn't have minded one bit if Marcus had said it was a date.

Chapter 10

Marcus walked next to Olivia on the beach. Ocean waves gently lapped at their feet. Overhead, a seagull begging for food played in the light breeze.

Choosing to be out with Olivia instead of alone in his apartment had been a good idea. Dinner had been outstanding. The food was top-notch, even if the restaurant was unique and not quite what he expected.

Knowing Chester had made the recommendation made sense. The restaurant was nice but casual since the wait staff wore pirate costumes.

Thankfully, Olivia thought it was fun. Next time, Marcus would check the website of any recommended restaurant, especially from someone as fun-loving as Chester.

"I enjoyed dinner." Olivia, carrying her sandals in her hand, grinned at Marcus.

"I'm grateful you have a sense of humor."

"It cracked me up when our waiter said, 'Ahoy mateys, I be Captain Jack Barrow'"

Marcus chuckled. "It was pretty funny. At least the food was good."

"It was great. And I loved that the waiter kept in character the entire meal. Makes me want to watch a pirate movie."

Surprised, Marcus glanced at her. "You like those?"

"Of course. My parents used to watch the old swashbuckling movies." She swished an imaginary sword.

A seagull screeched overhead.

Marcus motioned with his chin at the retreating bird. "I think he expected you to throw something with your arm movement."

Olivia glanced up. "Sorry, bird. I don't have anything to give you." She turned her attention back to Marcus. "I especially liked the movies where the women weren't completely helpless but were ready to fight the bad guys."

"You wouldn't wait for the hero to rescue you?"

"It would be nice, but there aren't many good guys these days. Why wait if I could fight for myself?"

Marcus raised an eyebrow. "You didn't take karate or ju-jitsu, did you?"

"No, unfortunately. But, it would be nice." She grinned.

"Well, I'd want to be one of the rescuing guys. Have the cool outfit and sword and come swinging on a rope across the deck of a ship to rescue the damsel in distress." He pictured himself swooping in to save the beautiful Olivia.

She giggled. "So, you want to be the hero?"

"Well, yes." He puffed out his chest. "Then the damsel would be in my arms, and I would take her to a place of safety. Our own little island in the South Pacific."

"You've thought a lot about this, haven't you?"

His chest deflated. "Maybe too much."

"I think it's sweet." She stopped walking and faced the ocean. "Being rescued and taken to a private island sounds really nice."

He stood beside her, watching the setting sun dip into the ocean.

She sighed. "It's beautiful, isn't it?"

He turned toward her. "Yes."

Olivia's gaze darted toward him. Even in the fading light, he could see her cheeks redden.

In quiet conversation, an older couple, holding hands, strolled past them.

Olivia turned her beautiful brown eyes toward him. "Have you ever been married?"

Marcus sputtered. Where did that thought come from? "No, I've never been married. How about you?"

She shook her head and started walking again.

He caught up with her. "That was a random question."

"Sorry about that, I was just curious."

"Anything else you would like to know?" He didn't mind her asking, but there were a few questions he hoped she wouldn't ask.

Swinging her sandals in her hand, Olivia's lips curled

up as she continued walking. "I'll think of something."

That comment pleased and terrified him.

Olivia felt like she was in a scene from a movie with the handsome man next to her. She couldn't remember a nicer evening. Being with Marcus at the restaurant and walking along the beach was perfect. She could easily picture Marcus as a swashbuckling rescuer. For him, she would gladly play the part of a damsel in distress.

Marcus stooped and picked up a shell. "It's still intact. Unfortunately, no pearl."

"That would have been fun." She kept pace with him as they continued walking. "You mentioned your mom was born in Puerto Vallarta. Did you spend lots of time there?"

"When we weren't traveling with my parents or in school, my sister and I would stay with our grandparents at their place overlooking the ocean. Alexa would run on the beach, and I'd surf."

"You can surf? I never wanted to go out very far into the water. Galveston is one of the closer beaches to Houston, and the water isn't as clear as it is here. Do you still see your grandparents?"

"No, they passed away. Two years ago, Abuelo had a heart attack, and Abuela left us six months later. Since they'd known each other for most of their lives, I don't think Abuela could stand being away from him for one more moment. While Abuela sat outside with her Bible on her lap, she looked at the ocean, and her heart stopped beating."

"I'm so sorry." How sad and yet beautiful that their lives were so intertwined.

"Yeah, I still miss them. I'm grateful I'll see them again one day when I get to heaven. My parents own the villa now. When dad isn't traveling, they spend time down there. They've fixed and modernized everything. Thankfully, the place still has the familiar touch of my grandparents."

"The villa sounds muy bonita."

Marcus stopped and gaped at her. "You know Spanish?"

She shrugged. "Solo un poco."

"Just a little, huh?"

"Sí."

"Mi hermosa amiga ¿te gustaría seguir caminando o regresar a Crawdad Beach?"

She swallowed hard. "Uh, I have no idea what you said other than Crawdad Beach."

Marcus chuckled. "I said, my beautiful friend, would you like to continue walking or return to Crawdad Beach?"

Olivia stared into his big brown eyes. "This has been

a wonderful evening, but we probably should get back since it's getting dark."

"May I escort you to my chariot, fair maiden?" He offered her his arm.

"Thank you, kind sir." She rested her hand on his muscular forearm.

He patted her hand. "I promise to keep you safe from every pirate we encounter."

"You are too kind and so very brave."

Enjoying walking with Marcus and the sounds of the ocean's gentle waves, she felt like she was in a sweet dream.

Back at her building, Marcus held her against his chest for a long, wonderful time. She could feel his heartbeat strong, steady, and fast.

He groaned, pulled away, and kissed her forehead. "Good night, Olivia."

She wouldn't have minded a kiss on the lips, not at all. But, if they were to stay friends, *just* friends, they would have to continue playing it safe. "Good night."

Olivia sank into her bed and sighed. What a perfect evening.

She hugged her pillow. Oh, how she hoped she would dream of a handsome swashbuckling Marcus coming to her rescue.

Chapter 11

Olivia changed from her sweatpants into her favorite well-worn, comfy jeans and a casual top. Since it was Saturday, Marcus had called and invited her to walk with him to the community park and a stroll by the river.

She was as ready as she could be for the opening on Monday and ready to enjoy as much time with Marcus as possible. She checked in the mirror one more time, then ran downstairs to wait by the door.

Even though it was a few minutes before eight o'clock in the morning, Main Street was already busy. An older man and woman powerwalked past her building. Outside Knick Knacks, a group of women stood waiting for the antique store to open.

Olivia grinned when her granddad peeked in her front window and waived. She stepped outside and locked the door behind her.

"Good morning!" Grandad hugged her. "What are you up to this fine morning?"

"Marcus and I are going to walk to the park."

"Excellent idea." Her Grandad smiled. "Marcus seems like a fine young man."

Oh, he is a mighty fine young man. Olivia bit back her grin at the thought. "What are you up to?"

"I'm going to have breakfast at Tiddlywinks, then help Katherine with her latest project."

"What is Aunt Katherine working on now?"

He pointed down the street to one of the few remaining empty buildings. "She's decided to convert the old Murphy building into a boutique hotel."

"Really? That's awesome. I knew she had discussed doing an event center or a hotel. I love the idea of having a hotel in Crawdad Beach."

"I think it should do well with all our town's visitors. Your mom hopes to help as much as possible."

"That's great. With Mom's years of hotel experience, she should be a great asset for Aunt Katherine."

"Crystal is still planning on helping you too."

She grinned at her grandad's thoughtfulness. "I know, but since I hired Jennifer, there won't be as much pressure for Mom to be involved unless she wants to be."

"Good morning!" Marcus, wearing jeans and a dark blue shirt, walked toward them and shook her grandad's outstretched hand. "Good to see you, Mr. Doss."

Her grandad smiled. "Likewise. So, you are escorting my granddaughter to the park?"

"Yes, sir. A clear, cool morning like this is perfect walking weather."

Grandad glanced at the sky for a moment, then smiled

at them. "It is a perfect day. You two have a nice time."

Marcus turned to Olivia. "You ready to go?"

"Excuse me!" An attractive woman with long, flowing silver hair hurried toward them. "Is this bakery open?"

"I'm sorry," Olivia said, "the grand opening will be Monday morning."

The woman sighed. "Oh, dear. I was hoping to buy some goodies to take back home."

"It will be worth the wait," Marcus said as he grinned at Olivia.

With a kind smile, the woman's green eyes surveyed them both. "That will be too late. I'm staying at the beach with a friend who is currently over at Knick Knack's shopping." She motioned with her hand. "We'll be checking out of our hotel on Sunday to return home, and it would be nice to have some snacks for our trip. "

Olivia bit her lip, wondering if she could spare a few things from the freezer. "I do have a few frozen cupcakes I could sell you."

"You do? That would be perfect and very appreciated."

Olivia unlocked the door and showed the woman inside as Marcus followed behind.

"Very nice." The woman stared at the decorations on the bakery walls. "You have done very well decorating your new bakery." The woman took her phone out of her purse and pointed it toward them as she took photos.

"I'll get the trays out so you can choose what you'd like." Olivia hurried to the kitchen while Marcus stayed behind, visiting with the woman.

Olivia brought out what she had and laid it on the counter.

"These are very nice. Would you mind if I bought a dozen?"

"No, that would be great."

The woman picked out a variety, and Olivia boxed up what the lady had chosen. She handed Olivia a fifty-dollar bill and a one-dollar bill.

Confused, she stared at the money. Thank goodness she went to the bank yesterday to have cash ready for the opening. "Let me get you some change."

"That won't be necessary. I appreciate you doing this for me. Consider it an early grand opening blessing. You can display the dollar as the first one you made with your new business."

"Well, thank you. That is very kind of you, Ms...."

The woman smiled. "I'm Stella Nicely."

"That's a nice name."

"I agree." Her smile brightened. "I couldn't have chosen a better one."

Olivia almost giggled at the lady's comment but kept her expression neutral. "I hope you enjoy the cupcakes."

"I know I will. Thank you, Olivia." With a mischievous glint in her eyes, she turned to Marcus.

"Marcus, you also have a great day. Enjoy your time together." With a wave of the hand, the woman left the building.

Olivia blinked and looked at Marcus, who seemed as confused as she was. "Did you tell her our names?"

He shook his head. "No, I didn't."

Olivia placed the money in her office safe. "Maybe she knows someone in town?"

"I don't know. The woman was pleasant enough while you were in the kitchen. She said she might move to Crawdad Beach because she had a very good friend who lived here. Then she smiled right at me."

"Strange. Either way, that was an unexpected, fun blessing." Olivia grinned at Marcus as she locked the door behind them. "I hope you didn't mind waiting."

"On the contrary. It was great watching you make your first sale as owner of Rolling in the Dough."

Marcus stayed next to Olivia on the side nearest the street as they walked along the sidewalk. Who was the woman who came to the bakery, and how did she know their names? Should he be worried? Maybe he was just being paranoid.

Something about her seemed familiar, yet surely he would remember someone who looked like her. Even though she was older, she was attractive enough to be a model.

He glanced over his shoulder. The lady was standing outside Knick Knacks. She smiled and gave him a slight nod. Marcus turned back to Olivia, took her hand in his, and picked up the pace.

She squeezed his fingers. "What's the hurry?"

He slowed down. "I'm sorry. I just saw that lady again."

Olivia grinned. "She did say she was here with a friend shopping."

"Yeah, I know. It's just strange the lady knew our names."

"It's a small town; anyone could have told her who we were."

"Maybe." At least he hoped Olivia was correct. He had enough problems trying to contain cyber-attacks; he didn't need a personal attack. He took a deep breath and decided to let it go and enjoy the day.

They arrived at the park. Birds sang in the trees above them, and flowers and crepe myrtles were still in bloom.

Olivia stopped by the play equipment. "When I was little, I came here with my mom and dad." A myriad of emotions crossed her face.

He gently squeezed her slender fingers. "Are you okay being here?"

"Yeah, sure. It's just strange, you know?" Her gaze

bounced to him, then back to the playground.

"I can't imagine."

"My dad was great. He loved my mom, and I never doubted that he loved me. I was fifteen when he died." She walked away.

He inwardly groaned. When he was fifteen, he was being an idiot hacker. He caught up with her. "I'm sorry. That must have been hard."

"It was awful." She stayed on the trail that led by the river. "We used to walk along here together. Mom and Dad and me."

"Olivia, if this is bringing back painful memories, we can do something else."

"No, it makes me sad, but it also helps me remember the good things."

"I get that. Life would be better for us all if we focused on the good instead of the bad." He mentally bopped himself in the head. Did that sound insensitive? He didn't mean it to.

She squeezed and released his hand. Stopping at a bench, she sat down, her gaze focused on the lazy river in front of them.

Marcus settled next to her. Sunlight glistened on the water. A frog croaked out a frog version of a song. He wasn't sure what to say, so he stretched out his legs in front of him.

"I'm tired of being angry."

He turned toward her. "Angry?"

Olivia didn't look at him; she swiped a tear from her cheek. "I've been mad at God for taking my dad."

"I'm sorry." He wanted to take her in his arms and tell her everything would be okay, but he wasn't sure if that was what she needed. His sister would get mad if anyone interrupted her when she was upset because she wanted someone to listen but not touch her until she finished processing. So, Marcus sat and waited.

Olivia took a shuddering breath. "I screwed up big time after Dad died."

"Losing someone you love isn't easy."

"I needed my dad. Mom is great, but I needed my dad."

Taking a chance, he slipped his arm around her shoulders and patted her.

Olivia laid her head against his chest and sobbed.

Chapter 12

Getting to her feet, Olivia wiped her face and tried to get herself back together. She couldn't believe she'd cried like that. Her tears came from losing her dad and losing pieces of herself because of her terrible choices.

Olivia rubbed her eyes. Marcus must think she's a basket case. "I'm sorry."

He stood next to her and dipped his head to get her attention. "Why are you apologizing?"

"I shouldn't have done that." She cringed when she noticed his shirt was wet from her crying all over him.

"Olivia, crying is a natural emotion that is good and cleansing. I've read that researchers say that crying helps flush out toxins and stress hormones. Better yet, God made tears, and the Bible says He puts them in His bottle. I think that's because He cares so much that every tear we cry is precious to Him."

"Well, my bottle must be pretty big by now."

Marcus put his arms around her and held her close. "I'm thankful you felt safe with me."

Olivia felt like something had shifted within her, relieving some of her anger at God. Maybe the tears had helped. The gentle sounds of the water flowing and playing along the riverbank further relaxed her tension.

Marcus's arms were around her, his heart beating against her. She clung to him, needing and loving his closeness. They hadn't known one another very long, but he did make her feel safe. Why couldn't she stay in his arms forever?

If only they had met sooner before she made all her mistakes. She didn't deserve someone as nice as Marcus. Olivia gently stepped out of his embrace. "Want to keep walking?"

"I would be honored to continue the journey with you." He kissed her hand like a gentleman in old England, then intertwined his fingers with hers.

Holding hands, they walked along the trail. Sunshine filtered through the trees above as a bird twilled in the distance. A squirrel chattered from a tree limb.

Marcus squeezed her fingers. "Are you excited about opening on Monday?"

"I am. The morning will be busy baking and getting everything ready. I just hope there'll be a decent amount of customers."

"I don't think you have anything to worry about. The Crawdadian population is great at helping one another, and I think most people in town have a sweet tooth."

"Good morning!" A young woman, with a lightning bolt shaved in her dark hair zipped past them.

"Hey, Alexa!" Marcus yelled at her retreating back.

"That was your sister, right?"

Marcus chuckled. "Yep, even when she was little, she was fast. In college, she set all kinds of track records. She excelled at sports, and I stayed focused on computers."

"You seem to have done alright. I bet you graduated college with one of those cum laude titles."

He shrugged. "Summa cum laude"

"Wow. I'm impressed. I only have a two-year degree from college and then an associate's degree in Culinary Arts."

"College *and* Culinary. Now, I'm the one impressed. One of my friends teased me that I had book smarts but lacked life smarts. And you know my cooking skills are extremely deficient."

"Other than your lack of cooking skills, you seem pretty smart."

"Thank you." Marcus stood taller. "I appreciate your misguided belief in me."

"So, you don't just wear your glasses to accentuate your good looks?"

"No. I'm blind as a bat without them. I envy those who can see the world without corrective lenses."

"You could get contacts?"

"Tried them." He cringed. "My eyes get too dry, and the contacts stick like glue to my eyeball." He made a sucking sound. "Not fun." Marcus handed her his glasses.

Olivia put them on and immediately got nauseous. "How do you see through these things?" She handed them back. "You really are just about blind."

He returned the glasses to his face and grinned her way. "I'll have you know that I can see just fine without my glasses as long as it is within six inches of my eyes. I never could accomplish the ping method, or echolocation, used by bats."

"You didn't really try that, did you?"

"Oh, yes. I did and drove my sister batty. No pun intended."

Olivia giggled. "Maybe that's why she started running."

"I hadn't thought about that." Marcus chuckled. "Maybe so."

In comfortable silence, they continued along the trail. She could get used to this. Marcus was so different from Geoff, who had never been chivalrous. On the contrary, Geoff had been impatient and rude. Why had she even dated him? Obviously, her vision had been severely impaired.

Coming to the trail's end, they turned around and headed back to the park.

Marcus squeezed her hand. "Are you up to joining me for lunch? I could drive us to the beach, find something to eat, then hang out."

"Food and hanging out sounds good to me."

"I was hoping you would say that. There's a great casual Mexican place right on the water. Would that be okay?"

"You're asking a native Texan if they like Mexican food? Of course, I like it. And that sounds great."

He adjusted his glasses and grinned. "Good. I also brought a blanket to spread on the sand and a few other necessities for beach bumming. So, after we eat, we could avoid diving seagulls and watch the waves."

"I like a man with a plan."

He leaned closer. "My plan is to spend as much time with you as possible."

She smiled. "Like I said, I like a man with a plan."

Stuffed to the gills, Marcus settled next to Olivia on the blanket he'd brought to the beach. Lunch had gone great, and they'd found the perfect spot to sit and view the ocean and people-watch.

An older man sat in a chair, occasionally calling to a dog romping in the waves. Further down the beach, a group of teenagers played beach volleyball. An overly built, overly-tanned guy jogged past and smiled at Olivia. Marcus narrowed his eyes at the man.

Shivering, Olivia wrapped her arms around herself.

Marcus moved closer and put his arm around her.

"Are you cold?"

Olivia leaned closer. "It is a little chilly."

"It's seventy degrees."

"I'm from Houston. Seventy is a cold front."

He chuckled, opened the canvas bag he'd packed, pulled out a light jacket, and draped it across her shoulders. "Better?"

She pulled it tight around her. "Much better. Thank you. You really did have a plan."

"Of course." He again put his arm around her. "My job entails calculating contingencies to prepare for anything. I brought a snack and water if you need anything else."

Olivia grinned at him. "I'm fine now. You have filled me with good food and salsa. What more could a woman want?"

Marcus tilted his head. "What more would *you* want?"

She raised an eyebrow. "That's a loaded question."

"Really? So, shoot away."

Olivia pulled her knees up and wrapped her arms around them. Her gaze moved to the ocean, and she sat quietly.

Should he say something else or wait for her to respond? Why would asking her what she wanted be a loaded question?

Maybe his friend was right; Marcus had book smarts but lacked life smarts, and he evidently also lacked women smarts.

Olivia glanced at him. "I'm not sure what I want."

"Oh." He mentally face-palmed himself at his lack of conversation skills. Why couldn't he write computer code to figure out things, especially women things?

She leaned closer, and her smile was a touch seductive. "What do you want, Marcus."

Gulping like a fish out of water, he adjusted his glasses. *What did he want?* He did not expect the question to return, and he sure would not share what he wanted since, at the moment, his thoughts were about Olivia and how beautiful she was. He glanced at her lips and quickly averted his attention to the ocean. "I want world peace."

She laughed. "Really? That's your answer?"

"Well, I've heard it before. It works in beauty contests, doesn't it?"

"I was hoping for something a little more personal."

"Hey, you didn't answer, so you need to cut me some slack."

"That's true." She gave him a wry smile. "I want world peace, too."

Oh, she was so beautiful. Marcus leaned closer, so close the scent of her subtle perfume wrapped around him. "You really want to know what I want?"

Her eyes widened, and she nibbled on her bottom lip.

Before he could react, she grabbed his shirt and planted a big, wonderful kiss on his lips.

She sat back and smiled. "Was that what you wanted?"

Her tone was riddled with amusement.

A nervous chuckle escaped him. "Well, yes, it was. Thank you for that. I appreciate your kindness."

"Well, I do want to be a kind person."

"In that case, kind woman, would you mind if I do this?" Marcus placed his hand behind her neck, gently pulled her closer, and kissed her, soft and tender, tasting the sweetness of her lips.

When he pulled away, her eyes were still closed. Well, if she was wanting more, how could he refuse? Lost in the moment, he reveled in the feel of their arms around one another and the taste of her lips.

Alarm bells? Was God sending him a danger signal? Pulling away from the embrace, he glanced around. The sound came from a fire truck passing on the street. Maybe God did send a warning signal before things got out of control.

Olivia stared at him with a dazed look, then smiled. "I do believe you have taken great steps toward world peace."

Chapter 13

Still smiling, Olivia moved closer to Marcus as they walked along the shoreline. She loved the feel of his fingers intertwined with hers. Besides being a wonderful man, Marcus was a great kisser.

Not far ahead, a group of partying teenagers danced and gyrated in an inappropriate manner to way-too-loud music.

Marcus squeezed her hand and guided her to turn around and walk the other way. Although his face still wore a pleasant smile, did he want a quieter walk, or did he think what the teenagers were doing was disgusting?

Regret pressed on Olivia's shoulders. She had done the same things as those teenagers when she was younger, and all it left her with were hangovers and regrets. Some people would think what she'd done was no big deal, but would Marcus want anything to do with her if he knew?

She figured God had to hate her for running around with the wrong crowd, drinking, experimenting with drugs, sleeping around when she was in high school, and then basically living with her old boyfriend. Sure, she'd heard all her life that God was forgiving, but why would he forgive her?

"I'm not sure God would forgive me." Olivia clamped her mouth shut. She didn't mean to say that out loud.

Marcus stopped and faced her. "Why would you say that?" His voice was gentle, not condescending.

Olivia wanted to crawl into a hole. Why did she say anything? They'd had a wonderful day together, and she'd just ruined it. Stupid regrets kept crawling out to attack her at the worst times.

"You don't understand. You have no idea what I've done." Why couldn't she keep her mouth shut? Why did she feel she needed to air her dirty laundry with someone she cared about?

Marcus stroked her cheek. "God is forgiving."

"Right." She huffed and avoided looking at him. "I know all that. But, I *knew* I was doing wrong things. I was so mad at God for taking my dad that I walked away from the church and my Christian friends and did things that still make me cringe. And then, for the last several years, I dated a guy who led me further away from God. My parents raised me in church. My grandparents, aunts, uncles, and cousins are all wonderful Christians. And me? I live in the same town but can never be like them."

His expression softened. "Do you think your family is perfect?"

She averted her eyes. "No, it's just that they have it together, and I don't."

"Olivia, we've all messed up." Marcus's deep voice was gentle. "I sure have. All through the Bible, we read the true-life accounts of those who lied, cheated, murdered, stole, denied Christ, committed adultery, and even were demon-possessed, and all were given God's grace and forgiveness. Whatever you've done, if you repent of those sins and go to Christ for forgiveness, He forgives."

Wishing she could absorb his confident faith, she raised her gaze to his. "You make it sound so easy. It's not." She'd heard it all before; even part of her believed it, but how could she return to God when she'd run so far away?

"I get it. I understand. Shame and guilt have kept many prisoners."

"You have one hacking thing you did at fifteen; that's no big deal." She walked away from him. Why was she being so honest with Marcus? Taking her heart out and exposing all the dirty, slimy, nasty things she'd done was a stupid thing to do. Why couldn't she just dive into the ocean and disappear?

Marcus caught up with her. "Olivia, my hacking *was* a big deal, but it's not just that I've screwed up in all sorts of ways. Do you want me to list my years and years of failures? "

"No. That's okay." She looked at his chocolate-brown eyes. "I can't believe we're having this conversation. We barely know one another."

Compassion filled his gaze. "Maybe that's why it's safe."

"Safe?"

"Yeah, we're both on a journey together. I won't throw stones at you if you don't throw stones at me for what I've done."

Olivia stared at the sand beneath her feet. "Good thing we are on a sandy beach and not a rocky shoreline."

Marcus took her in his arms. "You don't have to worry about the past. We've all messed up. And if somebody tells you they haven't, then they just lied. The Bible says *all* have sinned and fall short of the glory of God. That's why God's grace is so amazing. We all need forgiveness."

Part of her was thinking, blah, blah, blah, forgiveness, blah, blah, blah, because she'd heard it before. Why couldn't she believe it was true for her?

Marcus held Olivia against his chest. He understood the inner battle about forgiveness. It was hard enough to forgive someone who did wrong things against us, but when we're the ones doing wrong, forgiving ourselves seemed even more challenging.

He tilted her chin up to look at him. "I think I understand some of your struggles. I've had a hard time forgiving myself. The hacking job when I was fifteen, the relationships I've had in the past, the places I've gone, and the things I've done that were not God-honoring have kept me drowning in regret and guilt. As you said the other day, I've been a computer monk. It's easier to hide from the world and do penance for all the wrong things I've done. But self-punishment and isolation don't give relief and are not the answer."

"Okay, so are you planning on staying a monk and isolated?"

"No. Just the other day, I was thinking about how to forgive myself. The Bible says that when sinners came to God and genuinely repented of their sins, God would forgive them. I realized I needed to accept His forgiveness and stop beating myself up because His forgiveness removes our sins as far as the East is from the West."

Marcus gently turned Olivia to face the ocean and stood behind her. "We are now facing East." He maneuvered her to turn the other way. "Now we are facing West. The directions can never meet one another. Our sins are gone. God can not lie. So, when He says we're forgiven, our sins are gone."

Her gaze downcast, Olivia shook her head. "I don't know. I just don't know."

He held her against him and kissed the top of her head. "Memories of the ways we've screwed up should be used to help us not make the same mistakes again, but also cause us to be grateful for what God has done."

She didn't answer; just stepped out of his embrace and walked away.

Chapter 14

Through the night, Olivia tossed and turned. She'd bared her soul to Marcus and told him the stupid things she'd done. What he said about God and forgiveness made her want to believe that it was true.

At two o'clock in the morning, since she couldn't get to sleep, she threw off her covers and grabbed her robe. Opening the French doors, she stepped out on her balcony. The streetlights bathed the quiet sidewalk in a gentle glow. No cars, no people, the town rested in stillness. Why couldn't she rest? Clouds drifted across the moon above her.

Olivia moaned. She wanted to believe what Marcus had said. But, even if what he shared was true, she'd run so far from God that she didn't know if she could return.

"God, where are You? I'm searching for You, are You searching for me? Please find me." Her lip trembled, and she didn't bother wiping the tears running down her cheeks. "Please, forgive me, and help me forgive myself. I'm sorry. I'm so sorry."

She turned her face upward. "Where are You, God? I want You. I want to believe that You will forgive me. I want to come home to You." Sobs wracked her body as she stood in the moonlight. She sobbed, cried, and kept crying.

Olivia held up her hands. "Take them, take all my sins, take it all, and take me. Forgive me. Cleanse me. I want to come home to You."

A light breeze flowed across her face and her body, wrapping around her. She could sense, feel a release, a cleansing. In that moment, she knew her sins were gone as far as the East is from the West, and God had welcomed her home.

Chapter 15

In the foyer at church, Marcus looked over the heads of the people milling around him. Olivia said she would be here; at least, he hoped she would.

After their time on the beach, Olivia had wanted to go home. So, he had kissed her goodbye, returned to his apartment, and spent most of the night praying for her. He had prayed that whatever happened, he would do the right thing, whatever would honor God, even if it meant walking away from a relationship with Olivia.

"Good morning, Marcus. I hope you're doing well." Cane in hand, Henry Doss walked toward him. The man's radiant blue eyes gazed at him in a way that made Marcus feel like Henry could see in his soul.

"Yes, sir. Thank you."

"Waiting for someone?"

"I'm waiting for Olivia."

Mr. Doss smiled, "I was hoping you would say that. I spent most of the night praying for her and for you."

"You did?"

"Yes." Mr. Doss squeezed Marcus's shoulder. "Take good care of her." With that, he turned and walked away.

Marcus stood still. He had heard Mr. Doss was an amazing prayer warrior; did the man know something he didn't?

"Hello, Marcus." Chester slapped him on the back. "Good to see you, son."

"Thanks. Good to see you, too."

"You waiting for someone?" Chester gave him a mischievous grin.

His wife, Maybelline, took his arm. "Chester Taylor, leave the young man alone." She turned to Marcus. "Please forgive my ever-nosy husband. Hope you are doing well."

Marcus chuckled. "Yes, ma'am. I am doing well. Thank you."

Chester gave him a thumbs up as his wife led him into the sanctuary.

Crawdad Beach was definitely an interesting and entertaining place to live. Marcus grinned and went back to watching for Olivia.

The music started. Was she not going to come? Disappointed, he turned toward the worship center doors. He would keep praying for her.

A tap on his shoulder drew his attention.

Olivia, with a big smile, drew close to him. "I'm sorry I'm late." She took his hand. "May I sit with you?"

"I would love that." He took her hand and led her inside. Sitting next to her on a pew at the back of the church, he leaned close to her ear. "Are you doing okay?"

"I haven't felt this good in years." Her eyes looked sparkly, clean, and fresh.

"Really?"

Her smile grew as she nodded. "I'll tell you about it after church."

The congregation stood to sing. Olivia's sweet voice rang out clear and beautifully on-key, contrasting his croaking singing voice. Looking like the music enraptured her, she closed her eyes as she sang. He'd never seen her so beautiful.

Olivia couldn't remember a better church service. The music was wonderful, the Biblical sermon was encouraging and uplifting, and sitting beside Marcus made it even more special.

Why had she run from God, and why had she waited so long to return to church? She felt like she could breathe again and was alive. Even the birds this morning sounded like they were signing prettier tunes.

After the closing hymn, she grabbed Marcus's hand. "Can I make you lunch?"

"Thank you. That would be great." He kept her hand in his as they exited the church. "I'll walk you to your car. What time do you want me to come to your place?"

"Why don't you change into something a little more casual and come over when you're ready."

"Olivia?" Her mom, followed by Eric, ran toward her and enveloped her in a tight hug. "You're here! I'm so glad you're here."

Olivia chuckled. "Me too, Mom. Me too."

Eric grinned. "It's great to see you here."

"It's great to be here."

"Really?" Her mom's smile grew wider.

Olivia nodded. "Really, mom. It's all good now." She pointed toward the sky. "We're good now."

Her mom did a little dance. "Thank You, Jesus!"

Olivia laughed at the funny awkwardness of it all. Why had she waited so long to come back to God?

"Do you want to come over for lunch?" Her mom asked.

"Thanks, Mom. But I already have plans." Olivia smiled at Marcus.

"Oh, I see." Her mom's eyebrows danced. "Well, you two have a nice time. Olivia, we'll all be at the bakery bright and early in the morning to help with your grand opening."

"Thanks, Mom. It's going to be fun."

"Yes, it will." Her mom, with Eric's arm around her, walked away.

Marcus took her hand. "I am looking forward to lunch but even more so to find out how your evening was after

I left."

She grinned. "I can't wait to tell you."

At her apartment, Olivia changed into jeans and then hurried to finish the meal she had started early this morning, which was why she had run late to church. She still couldn't believe how much had changed in the last twenty-four hours.

Her phone signaled an incoming message. Marcus was waiting out front of the building.

Olivia rechecked the food, then hurried down the stairs and ran to unlock the door. She grabbed his hand, drew him inside, and gave him a quick kiss. "Come on"

She ran up the stairs with the sound of Marcus's footsteps behind her.

Once inside her apartment, she turned to him. "Did you know the verse about times of refreshing? Hold on, let me get my Bible." She giggled. "I can't believe I'm saying that. And it feels good."

She ran to her room, took the open Bible off her nightstand, and returned to where Marcus waited. "Check this out. In the third chapter of Acts, Peter was talking to a big crowd. He told them to repent and return to God so that their sins would be wiped away and times of refreshing would come from the presence of the Lord. Did you know about that? When we come to God, He wipes away our sins and leaves us with a feeling of refreshment.

Oh my goodness, do you realize how clean and fresh I feel now? Why didn't someone tell me about this sooner? I just felt guilty about everything and thought God hated me and didn't want anything to do with me."

Marcus chuckled. "God's grace is amazing and refreshing, isn't it?"

"Yes! I feel brand new. Squeaky clean, you know?"

"I can't tell you how happy this makes me."

"You too? It sure has made me happy. I should have called my mom this morning and probably the rest of my family. But all I could think about was telling you."

"Me?" His eyes got teary. "Why?"

"Marcus, you're the one that helped me connect the dots. I mean, I knew all those things, but something about the way you told me helped a lot." She put her arms around him and rested her head on his chest. "So, thank you."

His arms came around her. "I don't know when I've been happier."

She sighed. Being back with God and in Marcus's arms felt so right and so good. They might not have known one another very long, and she didn't care how he might react; she wanted him to know. "I love you, Marcus."

He tilted her chin up and gazed into her eyes. "I love you too, Olivia." The kiss he gave her was the best ever.

Chapter 16

Trying to tamp down her nervousness, Olivia adjusted her teal apron. She lovingly traced the bakery's name inscribed on the front. The grand opening was finally here. The licenses, inspections, and certificates for the employees and the business had been completed, and the bakery was finally ready to open.

Olivia glanced out the front windows. A line of people, including her family and Marcus, were already waiting on the sidewalk. She checked the cute custom clock she had ordered with the crawdad's claws keeping the time. In five minutes, they would open the doors.

"I'm so excited that it's finally here." Jennifer bounced on her toes as she stood behind the counter.

Olivia grinned. "I know. It's going to be great."

"I'm so proud of you." Her mom's arms came from behind and embraced Olivia.

"Thanks, mom." Olivia looked over her shoulder. Aunt Katherine, her cousin Tess, her cousin David's wife, Marie, Aunt Helen, and even Chester's wife, Maybelline, had all showed up at five o'clock this morning ready to help.

When the doors opened, Olivia and Jennifer worked as a team, helping and checking out customers and guiding and directing her family and friends on what needed to be done.

With a big smile, Marcus walked up and handed Olivia a vase of roses. "Congratulations on your first day."

She hugged him. "Aw, thank you." Olivia sniffed the beautiful flowers and put them at the end of the counter.

"You should have heard how excited everyone was out front as they waited." Marcus pointed to the glass-front display case. "Could I have one cinnamon roll, one blueberry muffin, and a cup of coffee, please?"

Olivia got his items and checked him out. "I'll see you this evening?"

"I'm counting on it." Marcus wiggled his eyebrows. "Don't worry about making dinner for me."

"I already have something started. I'll text you when it's finished."

"You are amazing, you know that?" His gaze went to her lips.

"Hey," Chester, in line behind Marcus, gave them both a mischievous grin. "You two need to finish flirting so the rest of us can get our sweet vitamin intake for the day."

Maybelline came out of the kitchen and playfully

shook her finger at her husband. "Chester, you behave."

"Aw, Maybelline, what's the use of behaving? I bet you don't want me to behave when I kiss you later."

Maybelline's face flamed red. "Shhh, not here."

Chester chuckled. "Seriously? You think these people don't know that we kiss?"

"Yes, but you make it sound like we're not behaving."

"We've been married for decades. We are blessed with guilt-free kissing and loving."

Maybelline fanned her face. "Oh, you are incorrigible."

Chester laughed and puffed out his chest. "And that's why you love me." While Maybelline looked like she would pass out, he turned to Olivia. "May I please have an éclair and a chocolate cupcake?"

Olivia giggled at the interaction between her friends. Maybe someday she would have a fun marriage like they did. She glanced at Marcus sitting at one of the tables, happily eating a cinnamon roll. He smiled and waved at her. When she turned back to Chester, he grinned but didn't say anything; he just grinned.

The line of customers kept coming. Some people picked pastries to eat at the bakery. Eric purchased a box of cupcakes for Doohickeys Hardware. Jeremy and Grace bought two cinnamon rolls and coffee to take back to Knick Knacks. The preacher bought a box of eclairs for the church staff. Even her grandad bought cupcakes for his great-grandchildren.

The next person to step to the counter was Stella Nicely, the lady who had come by Saturday morning.

The woman gave her a pleasant smile. "Good morning, Olivia. The cupcakes I bought the other day were fabulous, so I had to come back and see what else you had made. May I have a cinnamon roll along with a cup of coffee?"

Olivia nodded and laid the pastry on a plate. "I thought you were leaving on Sunday to return home?"

"I decided to stay longer. I'm meeting with a Realtor this morning to look around the area."

"Crawdad Beach is a great place." Olivia poured the coffee into a cup and handed it to Stella.

"I've heard many positive things about the town." The woman glanced over where Marcus was sitting, then returned her gaze to Olivia. "I think I could be happy here. I'm ready for a change."

Curious about why the lady looked toward Marcus, Olivia smiled. "I hope your house hunting goes well."

"I'm sure it will." Stella paid for the purchase, walked over to Marcus, pulled a chair across from him, and sat down.

If the woman had been younger, Olivia would be jealous. But still, she wondered who Stella Nicely was and what she was doing here.

Between serving customers, Olivia watched Marcus.

His face showed a variety of emotions, from surprise to smiles and then concern. They moved closer as if in a deep conversation, and then they both turned toward Olivia and smiled.

Olivia averted her attention back to helping those who were waiting in line. Just who was Stella Nicely?

By closing time, most of the bakery items had been purchased. Olivia closed and locked the door.

Applause and congratulations came from her helpers.

Her mom hugged her. "What a great day! Congratulations. I'm so proud of you. Everyone said they loved your bakery items."

Jennifer nodded. "They did, and you know what? I saw a lady typing something on her computer laptop. Later, Chester said she's a reporter for a local newspaper."

"Really?" Olivia said. "I hope she liked her pastries."

"Chester told me the reporter was excited and very positive about the bakery."

Maybelline grinned. "Chester does have a way of finding out most of what goes on in this town. Olivia, if it's okay with you, I'm going to recommend that my Bible study group meet here every Wednesday morning. Would that be okay? I'll make sure they know they have to buy something."

"Thank you. That would be great."

Olivia leaned against the display counter. It was such a great day. Everything went smoothly and without problems. She couldn't have asked for a better start for her business. Looking up at the ceiling, she sent a silent thank you to God.

The group helped her clean the bakery and prepare it for the next day. After they finished, Olivia thanked them, said goodbye, and locked the door behind them.

Now, she needed to enter the day's information into the computer and then get to the bank to make the deposit.

Once she got back, she'd get ready for her evening with Marcus and find out what Stella Nicely had said to him.

Marcus sure hadn't seen that one coming. True life was definitely stranger than fiction. Marcus shook his head. He would never have guessed that Stella Nicely was Dragon-Slayer58.

Since they had been online friends for years, even though he initially didn't know her age or gender, the relationship was still comfortable, mainly because Stella was an outstanding Christian lady whose faith reminded him of his grandmother's faith.

Stella asked Marcus to pray about an opportunity to work on a project together. They had talked for over an hour before she had to leave to meet her realtor.

Marcus had been thinking about what he needed to

do for several months, and now he knew. He would continue working for Dustin Bowman's firm here in town, but it was time to cut ties with his past life in Los Angeles. Marcus sent an encrypted message to his clients, giving them a two-week notice and a recommendation of who else they could use for their website security.

Taking care of those situations did make him feel like a burden had lifted. As far as what else Stella had offered, he needed to spend lots of time in prayer.

Chapter 17

"You made meatloaf?"

Olivia grinned at Marcus's broad smile as she entered his apartment. "Yes, I did. I also made mashed potatoes, green beans, and have cupcakes for dessert."

He followed her to his dining table. "How did you find time to do that? You were really busy today."

"I made the meatloaf in advance." Olivia put her delivery bag on the already set table and took out the dishes she'd brought. "All I had to do was put it in the oven when I closed the bakery."

"I'm impressed." Marcus moved out her chair, waited for her to sit, then hurried to his seat across from her. "I thought your opening went great. Were you pleased?"

"I was. We sold almost everything we had. Tomorrow morning, we will be busy trying to bake more inventory to sell. Thank goodness, I have lots of help."

"I think most of the town was there and many people I'd never seen before. Several ladies talked about how they had driven over from the beach."

"Speaking of ladies, who is Stella Nicely?"

Marcus grinned as he held out his hand toward Olivia.

"Let me pray first." His prayer was as sweet as usual, with the added thanks for Olivia's return to God. When finished, he squeezed her fingers and released her hand.

He handed her the serving spoon and waited for her to take a portion of the food, then served a huge helping of meatloaf for himself.

Olivia cleared her throat. "Are you going to tell me about Stella?"

"Oh, yeah. Sorry, I got sidetracked by your wonderful meal. I haven't had meatloaf in ages. Are you ready for this? Stella Nicely is Dragon-Slayer58."

"No! She's the hacker person?"

"Yep. And she's moving to Crawdad Beach." Marcus took a bite and moaned in pleasure.

"How do you feel about meeting her and finding out she's moving here?"

"At first, I was shocked. It still messes with my head that I had been in contact for years without knowing Dragon-Slayer was a woman. Stella may be older, but she's sharp and a great Christian. Her eyes can blaze right through you. She gave me some great advice, promised to keep us in her prayers, and made me an offer I'm considering."

"She knows about us?"

Marcus took another bite and nodded.

"So, what is Stella's offer?"

"It's a business proposition."

Olivia tried not to show it, but she was jealous that he had talked to the attractive woman for years. Good thing Stella was older because then there would be a real problem. "You're not going to tell me more about that?"

Marcus shrugged. "I need to pray and process before I make a decision."

What kind of proposition would Stella make? Olivia ate her meal while her overthinking kept overthinking. But she did still have questions. "Are you going to keep working for the company here?"

"Yep. I would just work with Stella on the side of my regular job."

"Won't that make you too busy?"

Marcus sat chewing for a few moments, then swallowed. "Probably not. I'm stepping away from my other moonlighting jobs. I've been meaning to cut those ties for months. Stella shared a couple of Bible verses that helped put things in perspective."

"Do you know where Stella lives now and where she'll live when she gets here?"

"She's in Bethesda, Maryland, said she's lived there most of her life. I mentioned how nice the loft apartments are, but Stella wants an older home she can tailor to her needs since a friend will probably move here with her."

"If Stella sells a home in Bethesda, she would probably make a hefty profit. That's close to Washington D.C., where home prices are expensive."

Marcus nodded. "Yeah, I guess so. I'm curious to see what she buys when she moves here. She lost her husband last year. I hate that I didn't even know."

"I thought you said you talked personal things with Dragon-Slayer."

"I did. But now that I think back, I was the one who shared personal stuff. Stella would gently nudge me back to the Bible and have me pray about whatever situation was worrying me. It's embarrassing now that I realize the conversations were pretty much one-sided."

Olivia shook her head. "And that statement comes from a man who makes his living on being observant with computer code."

Marcus cringed. "Yeah. Obviously, I need to work on my life skills." He put down his fork and sat momentarily, then leaned her way. "So, how are you doing?"

Olivia chuckled. "I'm fine. Thank you."

"Good. Um, any problems with the opening of the bakery? Need any help with anything? Anything else I need to know about or pray about?"

The poor guy was really trying to be more observant. "Okay, you can pray that I do the right things now that I'm back with God."

Marcus nodded. "Okay. I can do that. Yep. I can do that."

"Thank you. Now, are you ready for dessert?" She grinned as she handed him a cupcake.

"Always."

His cute smile made her heart feel all warm and fuzzy. Did a heart feel fuzzy? Was that really a thing, and would she want a fuzzy heart? Good grief. Her overthinking was back to overthinking.

How were they supposed to date and spend time together while keeping things platonic? And did platonic mean they couldn't kiss and hug and cuddle?

Where was the line drawn for Christian dating? Did that mean their relationship rating would have to stay G-rated, or could it be PG?

Since Marcus loved her, and she loved him, and they were over thirteen, did that mean they could date in the PG-13 range?

Oh dear. Whatever happened next, she better keep praying.

After eating another wonderful meal, Marcus sat next to Olivia on the couch. Putting his arm around her, she nestled against him.

Having Olivia near him like this was great. He could get used to this, but he needed to remember to be more observant, to continue praying for Olivia, and pray for himself that they would do the right things. Olivia was beautiful, had a great sense of humor, was a great cook, and was now back with God.

Besides praying about the relationship, he needed to make a list of dating ideas that would keep him out of trouble. The last thing he wanted to do was mess up either of their lives.

Olivia glanced up at him, and her lips looked ripe for a kiss. He did not resist kissing her, and she was happy to return his affection.

Marcus inwardly groaned. Dating Olivia and not taking things too far might be the hardest thing he's ever done.

Olivia pushed him away and got to her feet. Her eyes were wide. "PG, we need to stay PG."

"What?"

"Marcus, I love kissing you, but I think we need to stay at a PG rating."

He chuckled. "You mean like a movie rating?"

"Yes." She nodded and started pacing. "I love kissing you and your arms around me, and I love being around you, but oh, this is going to be hard to be good. Since we are over thirteen, maybe we could go up to a PG-13 rating, but maybe that would take things too far." She stopped and turned to him. "What do you think?"

Marcus stood and considered taking her into his arms, but he was still thinking PG-13 thoughts, so instead, he kept his distance. "I think you are wise. Maybe we could come up with some dating ideas that would be acceptable for a PG rating?"

Olivia nibbled on her lip and nodded. "Yeah, I think that would be good. I don't want to mess up being back with God. I wasted so much time and so many years that now I want to do the right things. But, I like you and love you, and you're so handsome and sweet and a great kisser." Her cheeks reddened, and she averted her gaze.

Marcus couldn't stand it; he had to be closer to her. He stepped in front of Olivia, took her hands in his, and looked into her big brown eyes. "Okay, let's make a pact for us both to work on this. I like and love you; you're beautiful, sweet, a great cook, and a wonderful kisser. We can't do this alone."

Her eyebrows rose. "You mean we need a chaperone?"

"Yes, probably. Instead, why don't we pray together."

Olivia shoved a stray hair behind her ear. "Both of us, right now?"

"Yes. I believe God brought us together. Let's pray He chaperones the relationship."

"Can we do that? Would that mean we have to stay at a G-rating?"

He chuckled, but that made him wonder, too. Was there a Bible verse on something like this? The only verse that came to mind was where Paul said to greet one another with a holy kiss. But he was talking about believers greeting one another. And, well, Olivia and he were believers, so maybe kissing would be okay. But keeping kissing holy would definitely put things into the G-rating.

Olivia squeezed his hands. "Do you want to pray first?"

Marcus bowed his head and prayed from his heart. God already knew his thoughts and desires. So, Marcus just let the prayer flow without worrying about what Olivia might think.

When he finished, Olivia prayed. Her sweet prayer made him want to stand taller, do the right things, and be the man God would want him to be for God, himself, and for Olivia.

Even with God's help, staying at a decent rating would be the most challenging thing Marcus had ever done.

Chapter 18

The last two weeks had flown by; business was going great, and dating Marcus was fantastic. Olivia hurried upstairs to get ready. Instead of cooking for Marcus this evening, he was taking her to dinner at his sister's house.

Olivia tried to fight off her nervousness. Other than seeing Alexa move at hyper-speed, Olivia hadn't had an opportunity to visit with Marcus's family. She had talked to Alexa's husband, Tony, a few times when Olivia picked up supplies for the bakery since he was the assistant manager at the grocery store. Tony was nice enough, but the man was intimidatingly massive.

After Olivia showered, she fixed her hair and makeup and chose her best jeans and a cute sweater top to wear. Marcus had told her to dress casual since he planned on them playing games with his nephew, Liam.

Ready with five minutes to spare, Olivia went downstairs to wait by the front door. She nibbled on her bottom lip. What if she said something wrong or they didn't like her?

Why was she so nervous? Then it hit her. When she dated Geoff, she had never met any of his family. Geoff had met her mom and friends, but why hadn't he introduced her to his relatives? The more Olivia thought about that relationship, the madder she got with herself. Why had she been so blind to how Geoff had treated her? And why was she thinking about Geoff?

Olivia looked out the windows. Marcus's SUV pulled into the parking place in front of the bakery. She locked up. When she turned, she grinned as Marcus opened the passenger door and waited for her. "Your chariot awaits."

"Is what I'm wearing okay?"

Marcus smiled and gave her a quick kiss. "Yes. You look great." He waited for her to buckle in before he closed the door and hurried to his side.

He slid in his seat and started the car. "Alexa said to warn you that her cooking skills are not great, so she made a pizza."

"I love pizza."

"Good, since it's Liam's favorite food."

"How old is your nephew?"

"He's four going on fourteen. He's a bright kid, and I'm not just saying that because he's family. Tony's parents are retired college professors who keep Liam when he's not in preschool."

"I was already nervous. Being around a mini genius will be even more intimidating."

"Why are you nervous?" He gave her hand a gentle squeeze. "They will love you."

"I hope so."

Marcus parked his SUV at a cute bungalow three blocks from Main Street and led her to the front door. "Don't be nervous. Just enjoy the evening."

Before knocking, the door opened, and Tony towered over them. "Glad you could make it." The big man shook Marcus's hand and then turned to her. "Welcome to our home, famous baker lady. Come on in. The pizza is almost ready."

"Uncle Marcus!" Liam ran and dove into Marcus's outstretched arms. Even though the boy was only four, he was tall enough to be an eight-year-old.

"Hey, buddy. I want you to meet a friend."

The boy flicked his gaze toward Olivia and then back to Marcus. "You mean girlfriend, right?"

"Right," Marcus said. "Olivia is my girlfriend. Can you say hello?"

"Of course, I can say hello." His comment wasn't rude; it was more like he was surprised that Marcus would even think Liam couldn't address her. "Miss Olivia, it is very nice to meet you."

She nodded toward him. "Thank you, Liam. It is very nice to meet you, too."

Alexa, wiping her hands on a dishtowel, zipped toward them. "Olivia, I'm glad you could join us for dinner."

"Thank you. I appreciate the invite."

Laim squirmed out of Marcus's embrace and took Olivia's hand. "Come on, I want to show you what I've been working on."

Olivia glanced at the adults as Liam led her away. "I'll be back with you later."

Still holding Olivia's hand, Liam opened a door. "This is my room," he exclaimed proudly.

Surprised at his neatness and the level of complexity of his toys, she smiled at him. "Your room is very nice."

"Thank you. Actually, I still have work to do to finish my Lego space station." He pointed to the structure that looked like a team of adults had assembled. "You built this by yourself?"

He blinked up at her. "Of course. I have been working on this since I was younger."

Olivia bit back a laugh. "Oh, I see."

"Yes, now that I'm older, I understand physics better."

She nodded. There was no way she would tell him she still didn't understand physics.

"Dinner is ready." Grinning, Marcus stood in the doorway. "Liam, would you be so kind as to escort Miss Olivia to the table?"

"Yes, sir." The not-so-little boy escorted her to the dining area and pulled out a chair for her.

She sat. "Thank you, Liam."

"You are most welcome."

Marcus sat next to her and leaned close. "He's pretty

sharp, huh?"

"He's incredible."

During dinner, Alexa shared funny stories about their childhood. Tony told a humorous story about her cousin, David, when he first met his wife, Marie. And Liam explained what he had learned about the process of a caterpillar becoming a butterfly.

After they finished, Alexa asked Olivia if she wouldn't mind helping her in the kitchen.

Olivia picked up the plates off the table and followed Marcus's sister.

Alexa turned toward her and crossed her arms. "I would like to know what your intentions are with my brother."

Olivia gulped. Did Alexa not like her? Was she mad Marcus was dating her? "I care for him and hope we will have a future together. I really like him. He's a very nice guy."

Alexa's eyes narrowed. "Do you love him?"

"Yes, I do love him."

"Good. You have answered correctly." Alexa grinned, then laughed. "I wish you could have seen your face." Alexa enveloped her in a big hug. "Welcome to the family."

Olivia stood there with her arms by her side and then patted Alexa. Was this some sort of strange family initiation?

Still chuckling, Alexa released her. "Sorry about that. I just wanted to have some fun. I know Marcus cares for you. Actually, I know he loves you."

Olivia bit her lip to stop it from trembling. Marcus loved her and even told his sister he loved her.

"Are you messing with my girlfriend?" Marcus gave his sister a stern but playful look.

"Of course I am. What kind of sister would I be if I didn't make sure Olivia had your best interest at heart."

The smile he gave Olivia made her knees weak. Knowing that she was loved and Marcus wanted others to know he loved her was amazing.

They moved to the family room, where she sat beside Marcus on Tony and Alexa's brown sectional. The room was comfortably decorated with an eclectic furniture group from traditional to modern.

Liam disappeared and then returned with video game controllers. "Uncle Marcus, you are two games behind me, and you promised to try to beat me." Liam chuckled as though that would be impossible.

Marcus stood and walked to where the boy waited. "You are right. Plug them in, and I will show no mercy this time. The winning game will be mine."

Liam giggled. "I would like to see you try." He turned to Olivia. "Would you like to join us?"

Olivia shrugged. "I don't know. I'm not very good at video games."

The boy came toward her and gave her a gentle look. "I will help you if you need it."

How could she refuse? Olivia sat beside Marcus on the floor. She knew she was over her head two minutes after the racing game started. But that didn't matter; she was having a great time with Marcus's family.

Marcus tried to beat Liam, but the kid was too good and too fast. From the determined look on Olivia's face, she was trying hard to keep up with them. He probably should have warned her before they arrived that Liam had beaten every video game he owned. Of course, Tony and Alexa ensured Liam had only decent games to play.

Olivia fit in great with his family. Alexa and Tony had both whispered to Marcus their approval and the fact that Liam immediately took to Olivia spoke volumes.

"Nooooo." Olivia groaned as her video car wheels fell off, and she was stuck on the roadway.

Liam paused the game and patted her arm. "It's okay. I'll send a tow truck back to help."

She smiled. "Thank you, Liam."

With the flick of Liam's fingers, he pushed the buttons of his controller, and a menu appeared. He scrolled through and pushed buttons again, and sure enough, a little tow truck came flying into the game to help Olivia's car.

Marcus shook his head. He didn't know you could do that. How did Liam know?

A few minutes later, they were back in the race.

Olivia's car flew past Marcus, leaving him in the dust. She cackled an evil-type laugh.

He turned to her. "Hey, how did you get so fast?"

Liam giggled. "I supercharged her car."

"You did?" Marcus playfully narrowed his eyes at his nephew. "That's not fair."

Liam gave him a look that said he was not amused. "Life is not fair. You better get used to it."

Olivia laughed. "Yeah, Marcus. You better get used to it."

Marcus chuckled. Man, he was so in love.

Chapter 19

Olivia stood at her stainless steel worktable in the bakery kitchen, working on a three-tier wedding cake. She would miss seeing Marcus this evening, but after dating for over a month, keeping their dating rating at a decent level was getting more and more difficult.

The cooler weather now limited their outdoor time. Not that it was horribly cold; it was just that she didn't like being chilly. So, she and Marcus had spent time with friends and family so they wouldn't be alone as much. They ate out at restaurants, watched movies, and even spent evenings playing video games with Liam.

Today, after work, she was going to visit with her grandad while Marcus worked on the computer project at Stella's house. Even though Marcus had explained what they did together, Olivia didn't understand the cybersecurity computer lingo. All she did know was that they were working on some kind of software code to help protect websites from attacks.

While Jennifer helped with customers, Olivia stayed busy decorating the cake that would be picked up before they closed for the day. Would she ever have the blessing of a wedding? Marcus loved her, but they hadn't discussed long-term plans for their relationship, which wasn't something Olivia felt she should discuss. Not yet, anyway. However, the very pleasant thought of having Marcus as a husband often crossed her mind.

Olivia focused on cake decorating and fashioning the customer's requested buttercream flowers.

Jennifer walked toward her. "The cake looks wonderful. The last customer left, so I locked up the bakery for the day. I'll get everything cleaned up while you finish decorating."

"Thanks." Olivia stepped back from the cake. "Do you think the client will like it?"

"She will love it! I know her and her fiancé. They both grew up in Crawdad Beach and now work at Lawson Manufacturing. At their wedding, they'll replace their purity rings with their wedding rings."

"Purity rings? You mean like they stayed pure and didn't, you know...?"

Jennifer nodded. "Amazing, huh? Especially in this day and age."

Olivia inwardly cringed. With her many past mistakes, if she ever got married, her wedding dress should probably be a dingy gray color.

Why was she thinking that Marcus would want to marry her? And why would God be kind enough to bless her with a husband like Marcus? God had already been much kinder than she deserved. Olivia did pray for Marcus and their relationship, but maybe praying that he would ask her to marry him would be asking God for too much.

No, she didn't deserve anything else from God. The fact that He let her back into His good graces was more than enough. She didn't deserve a happy-ever-after.

"Are you sure?" Marcus stood behind Stella as she stared at her computer screen.

"I'm positive." She looked up at him and grimaced. "This isn't good. The code is embedded so deep, it would take us a month to get it removed."

Marcus rubbed the back of his neck. "At least we know where the breach is in the software."

"Yes. I'll send a message to my friend thanking him for the friendly but destructive hack."

"I appreciate his help, but it puts us back to square one."

Stella shrugged. "That's part of the process. If we don't thoroughly test the software, it will only cause trouble for our clients. We can use the previous backup and start from there to close any access points hackers might use."

"Right." Marcus took another look around Stella's

incredible office. The craftsman house she had bought looked ordinary outside and in the tastefully decorated main living area, but her secure area had an entirely different appearance. The room had the latest computer technology, along with surveillance camera feeds showing every angle of her house, reminding him of what he'd seen at a government covert facility.

Stella's piercing eyes gazed at him. "I'm sorry to keep you from Olivia."

"No, it's okay. She's going to see her grandad this evening."

"Are things getting serious? You two make a very nice couple."

"We haven't dated very long, so I guess I shouldn't rush, but I hope we have a good future together."

Stella smiled. "I was ready to marry my husband a week after we met."

"How long did you date?"

"Seven months, four days, and five hours." She gave him a sly grin. "Not that I was counting. We were both in the military and married for forty-five wonderful years. I still miss him. We always thought I would be the first one to go since..." She turned away and waved a dismissive hand. "Forget I said anything."

Marcus didn't press, but he sure was curious. What did she almost share?

Interesting. Stella Nicely had secrets.

Chapter 20

Shoving her hands in her jacket, Olivia walked along Main Street's sidewalk. Turning the corner, she made her way to where her grandad lived.

She couldn't get the fear out of her head that all the good things happening in her life would blow up in her face since she'd done so many bad things. Olivia sighed. Why couldn't she have stayed on the straight and narrow and be wearing a purity ring instead of feeling like she was trashy used goods?

Marcus had a past he wasn't proud of, so he wasn't the one making her feel guilty, but still, Olivia felt like a dark cloak of shame was pressing down on her. She'd returned to God; why did she lose her warm fuzzy and clean feeling? What happened to her times of refreshing?

Her grandad would know how to advise her. Talking to him always helped. No matter what she told him, he never got upset or angry or told her what a bad person she was; he always loved her. She knocked on his door and waited.

He welcomed her inside. "How are you doing?"

Olivia pasted on a smile. "Everything is going really

well. The bakery is doing great, and dating Marcus is wonderful."

His head tilted. "But?" He pointed to the couch and waited as she sat down. Her grandad always seemed to have a sixth sense, or maybe it was his amazing God-connection. He settled next to her and waited.

His little dog, Filbert, wagged and sat at her feet.

She gave Filbert some love, then looked in her grandad's kind eyes. "I don't deserve all these nice things. I keep wondering if God will strike me with lightning or make me pay for all the times I didn't do the right things."

He sat quietly momentarily and then gave her arm a gentle pat. "Do you remember when you were a little girl, your grandmother and I visited you and your parents in Texas, and you showed us your toy kitchen?"

"Yeah, I loved that little playset." She had baked many imaginary meals. Of course, they all had been masterpieces.

"What happened the day you broke off the handle on your toy oven?"

Olivia wrinkled her nose at the memory. "I had gotten mad because I'd spilled mud pie all over my shirt."

"You had quite a temper that day. What did your dad do?"

"He fixed the handle for me." Even as a little girl, she knew her anger had caused the problem. But still, her dad kindly knelt in front of her, helped her clean her shirt, and then fixed her playset.

"Your father's love didn't stop because of what you had done. Even more so, God's love never fails. I gave you the building, apartment, and bakery because I love you and want the best for you. God's love, forgiveness, and grace are far bigger and more amazing than human love. You've trusted God to save you. Now trust Him for whatever comes next."

Could God love her even with all the ways she'd failed? Could it be so simple and so true? "But, I'm not where I need to be. I have so much to learn and feel like I've lost my chance at happiness."

"Your lost years can't be replaced, but God has given you a new future."

"Grandad, I love what you've given me, and I'm in love with Marcus, but what if all that is taken away and I lose a happy-ever-after with Marcus because of what I've done?"

"What does the Bible say about our sin when we go to God, repent, and ask for forgiveness?"

Olivia thought of her earlier conversation with Marcus. "God forgives us, cleans us up, and throws the sin as far as the East is from the West."

Her Grandad smiled. "Correct. God forgives and no longer remembers that sin."

She swiped a tear from her cheek. "But what about the people in the Bible who had bad stuff happen after they became Christians? And why did my dad have to die? He was a good Christian."

Grandad handed her a tissue. "We live in a fallen world. Life will be difficult, but it does not mean God isn't loving. We prayed for your dad's healing, but sometimes healing comes in heaven." He paused and patted her hand. "As for your earlier comment about not being where you need to be. We are all a work in progress." He smiled gently at her. "Do you remember when you were a little girl, and we went blueberry picking?"

Despite her tears, she smiled. "Yes, that was a fun day."

"We found ripe blueberries on the same branch where others were still green," Grandad continued. "Sometimes, the ripest berries were found under a leaf or in the bush where the sun barely reached. Olivia, God's people are grafted into God's vine, but it doesn't mean they mature at the same speed. Even green blueberries will ripen as long as they stay connected."

Olivia shredded the tissue in her hand. "I'm barely at the green stage. I lost so many years doing things I shouldn't have done. Sure, I had a job and did well as a pastry chef, but I didn't honor God in how I lived."

"Other than Jesus Christ, there isn't a person on earth who hasn't sinned. Please don't allow the devil to keep you chained to what God has forgiven you for. And Olivia, enjoy the blessings God has given you."

Filbert, lying at their feet on the wood floor, lifted his head and wagged.

Olivia patted the little dog. She kept beating herself up for something God had already forgiven. What good was it looking back at her mistakes that could never be changed?

She needed to stop letting the devil chain her to something that God's forgiveness had cut and freed her from.

Chapter 21

Be careful.

Back at his apartment, Marcus kept pondering the last thing Stella said. Was she referring to his job, their project, Olivia, or living in Crawdad Beach? When Stella's intense gaze bored into his, he should have asked her what she meant instead of just giving her a nod as he left her house.

Now, he was feeling paranoid. He had made a few enemies when he took down hackers. He checked the locks on his doors and windows to ensure everything was secure. The software project with Stella shouldn't be an issue since it wasn't even available to the general public.

What was he thinking? Crawdad Beach was probably the safest place Marcus had ever lived. He kept off social media and made sure anything personal was not on the internet. As much as possible, that is, since there were ways to track someone.

Curious, he sat at his computer and typed in his name for a deep-dive search on the dark web. He groaned as more information than he could imagine appeared on the screen. So much for staying behind the scenes.

With his computer skills, he could remove most of the

data, but who might have already seen what had been online?

The alarm on her phone sounded. Groaning, Olivia rolled over in bed. Four-thirty was way too early, but she needed to get moving. The bakery items wouldn't get made by themselves. Why couldn't elves do the work for her?

Mumbling to herself, she took a shower, dressed, and went downstairs. She shouldn't complain. Life was going great. Her bakery continued to be profitable, and dating Marcus made her feel like she was living a true-life fairy tale.

Since she talked to her grandad, the heaviness of shame had lifted. To keep that guilt monster off, she kept repeating the verses that said it was for freedom that Christ set us free, and there is no condemnation for those who are in Christ Jesus. She was forgiven, free, and not condemned. Olivia turned off the alarm and flipped on the lights. Jennifer had a key to the back door and should be here soon.

Olivia paused as she looked around. She loved the building, apartment, and bakery her grandad gave her. Even though he insisted Olivia didn't owe him anything, she planned to give him a check to start repaying his generosity.

The back door opened, and Jennifer came inside. "Good morning!"

"Good morning. Ready to start baking?" Olivia put on the coffee.

"Yep. Do you have the list for today?" Jennifer followed Olivia into the kitchen.

"I do." Olivia laid her recipe cards so they could both read them, then turned on the ovens to get them warm.

Jennifer yawned as she took out the baking supplies needed and placed them on the worktable. "Did you have as much trouble getting up as I did this morning? Maybe it's because the weather is cooler, and being warm and comfy in the bed makes it hard to get up."

"I agree. I hope the coffee is finished soon."

"Yoo-hoo! We're here." The cheery sound of Maybelline's voice came from the other room.

Maybelline, followed by Olivia's mom, Tess, and Marie, entered the kitchen. Greetings were exchanged, and they put on their aprons and got to work.

Happy chatter filled the room as they prepared the items for the morning.

"Olivia, I have a favor." Maybelline stood next to her. "Chester's birthday is tomorrow, and I want a special cake made for him."

"I would be glad to do that. What kind would you like me to make?"

"His favorite is just a simple lemon Jello cake. You know, the ones where you use a toothpick and pour lemon Jello in it. I want you to decorate the top with something out of the ordinary. Not just happy birthday."

Olivia grinned. "Out of the ordinary?"

"Yes. I want Happy Birthday Chester on it, but I also want a Shetland pony, an army guy, and a magnifying glass."

"Okay.... That sounds different."

"I better explain. When Chester was a teenager, he was a Shetland pony wrangler. After college, he joined the army and was an intelligence officer."

"Really? Wrangling Shetland ponies? That's really a thing?"

"Oh, yes. Those little horses have quite an attitude and are almost as ornery as Chester."

Thinking about Chester and ponies and him being an intelligence officer, Olivia muted her laugh with a cough. Why didn't she know all this sooner? And what else didn't she know about the people in this little town?

When the bakery opened for the day, Chester moaned as he slowly walked to the counter. "Food. Must. Have Food."

Olivia handed him a cupcake and a cup of coffee.

He gave her a pitiful look. "Thanks. I was weak from hunger."

"I bet you haven't eaten since last night at dinner."

He took a drink of coffee and nodded. "It's been hours."

Maybelline strolled out from the kitchen and sighed. "Chester Taylor, you are so dramatic."

He gave her a sheepish look. "Hi, darling. I've missed you." Chester turned to Olivia. "You know we met on a blind date. And she's been blind ever since because otherwise, there is no way she would put up with me all these years."

Maybelline chuckled as she returned to the kitchen.

Chester grinned. "She's a good woman." He set his food and drink on the counter and handed Olivia money. "Things going well with Marcus?"

"Yes, things are going very well." Olivia grinned as she gave Chester his change.

"The town is rooting for you two."

"Rooting, huh?"

Chester's gaze turned serious. "Yes, that means we are cheering for, supporting, and believing in y'all."

She giggled. "I know what it means. It just sounded funny."

He chuckled. "Oh, okay. Well, we will keep rooting and praying."

"Thank you. We need all the rooting and praying we can get."

The rest of the day zoomed by with the steady stream of customers. With Thanksgiving coming in another week, the orders for pumpkin pies and other desserts were stacking up and would keep them busy until the holidays were over.

After work, Olivia hurried upstairs to her apartment to make a meal for Marcus. She couldn't wait to tell him about her time with her grandad and find out about Marcus's time with Stella.

An hour and a half later, Olivia placed the dishes she'd brought on his table.

Marcus hovered beside her. "What did you bring?"

"Tonight we're having Chinese Chicken Salad."

His nose wrinkled. "Chicken salad like the mayonnaise stuff?"

Olivia chuckled. "No, silly. This is made with chicken, lettuce, red cabbage, mandarin oranges, crushed ramen noodles, carrots, green onions, sliced almonds, and a Chinese dressing."

"Okay. Good. That sounds great. I like regular chicken salad, but not if it has too much mayonnaise." He shuddered.

She grinned. "I will make a note of that."

After enjoying the meal together, they sat on the couch.

Olivia cuddled next to him. "Chester said the town is rooting and praying for us."

Marcus put his arm around her and drew her closer. "How can we lose? When the Crawdadians are rooting and praying, good things happen."

She liked how that sounded but still wasn't sure what Marcus had in mind for the future. "Are you going to see your parents over Thanksgiving?"

"No, mom and dad are in Italy for a few more weeks."

"Italy? Are they on vacation?"

"Let's just say that Dad travels overseas for work, and Mom often accompanies him."

Olivia nudged him. "Sounds like spy stuff."

Marcus chuckled. "You have quite the imagination, don't you?"

"I bet if I asked you point blank, you would say that you would neither confirm nor deny my idea."

Marcus sat quietly for a moment. "So, how was your day."

She squirmed out of his arms and looked him in the eye. "I knew it. Your dad and possibly both your parents are spies."

He sighed. "I will neither confirm nor deny your suspicions."

Olivia nuzzled against him. "This is so exciting. I've never met the son of a spy before."

Marcus's arms enveloped her. "How would you know that you haven't already met one?"

"Good point. I guess that's not something most people talk about freely. Is there some code that family members have to go by? You know, like a secret handbook you must read and destroy?"

"Definitely. I can't tell you how many documents I've had to destroy after reading."

"Really?"

Marcus laughed. "No. I can't tell you because there are no documents."

"Are you making fun of me?" Olivia squirmed and sat in front of him. Narrowing her eyes, she moved closer. "Will I have to torture you to tell me the truth?"

His eyebrows rose along with his lips. "Do your best, woman. I will never talk."

Olivia cracked her knuckles and attacked.

Chapter 22

Laughing so hard his stomach was cramping, Marcus held up his hands in surrender at Olivia's tickle attack. "Stop. Mercy. Please have mercy."

She looked rather smug as she surveyed him. "So, you give up?"

"Yes, torture me no more. I am powerless against you. I'm fading fast, and the only thing that will help is..." He took a deep breath like it was his last. "Is mouth-to-mouth resuscitation."

Olivia giggled. "You poor thing. I would hate to lose you." She wrapped her arms around him, and her lips met his.

He was more than happy to take full advantage of her willingness. The kisses started slow and sweet, then went deeper and quickly turned into smoldering passion. He could easily get lost in the moment. Expecting the fire alarm to go off at any moment, he pulled away. His thoughts were going in far too many ways they shouldn't.

She grabbed his shirt and pulled him closer. Her lips skimmed his. "I do believe I won this round."

Marcus raised an eyebrow as he looked into her

beautiful brown eyes. Olivia knew too well how to play the game. As much as he wanted to continue, he knew the regrets would linger. He stood and offered his hand. "You have won, my lady. I am yours."

Olivia let him pull her off the couch, and she snuggled in his arms. "Thank you."

He kissed the top of her head. "For what?"

"I haven't had that much fun in forever. Thank you for being a gentleman."

"It was fun, and you're welcome. It's sure not easy to be a gentleman."

She giggled and hugged him tighter. "It is definitely *not* easy to be a lady."

Marcus groaned. "I think we should eat our meals somewhere with lots of people and avoid alone time."

Olivia sighed. "As much as I hate not to have you all to myself, I think that's probably a wise idea."

Having her in his arms, pressed against him, felt so right. Before his thoughts went where they shouldn't, he stepped out of the embrace and took her hand. "I better walk you home."

"Yes, please." Humor lit her eyes. "The mean streets of Crawdad Beach are out there."

"The crawdads do come out at night." Marcus narrowed his eyes and leaned toward her. "Thousands and thousands of them crawl the streets after midnight."

Olivia's eyes went wide. "Okay, you're creeping me

out." She pulled him toward the door. "Take me home."

"Don't worry, it's only nine o'clock."

"I know you're teasing, but the visual you gave is very disturbing. You were teasing about the crawdads, weren't you?" Her gaze searched his.

Marcus laughed. "Yes, I was joking." He led her down the apartment stairs and stopped when they reached the sidewalk. "See, not one crawdad anywhere."

"I don't know." She walked next to him. "Since we live in town, we are Crawdadians."

Man, he loved Olivia's cute humor. "I'll protect you from any crawdads and Crawdadians."

"You are my hero." She giggled as she entered her security code to turn off her building's alarm. Finished, she placed her key in her door and turned toward him. "Want to come inside for a few minutes? Check around and make sure no crawdads crawled in while I was away?"

Seeing Olivia in the soft glow of the streetlights made her even more beautiful. Stifling a moan, he blew out a breath. "I think you would be much safer if I went back to my place." He gave her a quick kiss and waited until she was safely inside.

Marcus returned to his apartment and checked his computer. A message popped on his screen.

He sucked in a breath, hurried to his bedroom closet, and opened his safe. He took out his holstered nine-millimeter handgun and slid it inside the waistband of his pants. Putting on a jacket, he said a quick prayer for protection and rushed out the door.

Chapter 23

Olivia checked her phone for the fourth time and returned it to her jean's back pocket. She still hadn't heard from Marcus. He usually texted her in the mornings. Maybe the crawdads got him before he got back to his apartment. She chuckled at the thought, then creeped herself out, thinking about what that would really be like.

Hopefully, he was busy with some cybersecurity issues, and time got away from him. She might have to tickle attack him this evening to teach him a lesson. Olivia fanned her face at the thought.

"Are you hot?" Her mom stood beside her. "Maybe you should step away from the ovens."

Olivia turned her attention to check the timer. "I just was seeing how long before the cakes were ready."

Her mom grinned. "Right. I think you might have been thinking about Marcus."

"He does tend to invade my thoughts every now and then." Why hide it? She was in love.

"I'm sure he does." Her mom snickered as she returned to help Jennifer with customers.

The oven timer sounded. Olivia pulled out the pies

and set them on the cooling rack. She still needed to decorate three cakes. Tess had helped early this morning but left at eleven to have lunch with her children at their school. Olivia shook her head. It was strange that both of her cousins were married with children.

Would she ever have kids? With Marcus's Latin heritage and the Asian blood of Olivia's grandmother, their babies would be super cute. Olivia shook off the thought. They hadn't talked about marriage, but she did hope the relationship would move in that direction.

Olivia took out her phone and checked again. Bummer. Still no word from Marcus.

"You need to get back home."

Stella's voice jolted Marcus from a weird dream. He blinked and forced open his eyes as he shifted in his chair. "What time is it?" He ran his hand through his hair and yawned. Gag. His teeth felt like they were covered in fuzzy socks.

"It's one o'clock." Stella handed him a cup of coffee.

"I thought it was later." He took a sip of the warm liquid, hoping it would make his groggy head more alert.

"That's one in the afternoon." Stella grinned and sat at her computer keyboard.

"What?" Marcus jumped to his feet, almost knocking

over his chair. "How long have I been sleeping?"

"You fell asleep about four hours ago."

No wonder his back hurt. "I'm sorry." He stretched. "I should have stayed awake."

"No worries. Everything is fine. My friend arrived two hours ago."

"You should have told me what you were involved in."

Stella turned toward him. "You should know that some information is shared only when sharing is needed."

Marcus nodded. He knew that all too well with his dad's line of work. Olivia had guessed correctly on a few things. "So, is the threat level over?"

"Yes. My friend took care of the situation."

In her line of work, he wasn't sure he wanted to know how that was rectified. "Well, I better get home."

Stella stood. "Thank you for coming over last night."

"I'm glad you called me."

"I wanted to ensure I knew where you were while handling the situation."

"Wait, so you didn't need my protection?"

Her eyebrows raised. "You should know better."

Marcus felt his shoulders sag. So much for any of his thoughts about being a hero.

Stella's intense green eyes surveyed him. "Your dad was right; you are a very fine young man."

Marcus felt like the earth shifted under his feet. "My

dad? You know him?"

Stella chuckled. "Of course. I've worked with him for years."

"Why didn't you tell me?" He grabbed the back of the chair to stabilize himself. "That makes our friendship even weirder." Marcus let out a groan. He would die of embarrassment right here and right now.

Stella's smile was kind. "Your secrets are safe with me. I value our friendship, Marcus. You have nothing to worry about."

"That's easy for you to say." Marcus sat in the chair and put his head in his hands. "I shared things with you that I would never have shared with you if I had known it was you, and you knew my dad." He had to get away. Far away. Maybe he could get Olivia and head off to a private island in the Caribbean.

"Marcus, your father is a special friend. Thirty years ago, he saved my life when we were on a mission together. I would never do anything to hurt a member of his family."

He jerked his head up. "My dad saved you?"

"Yes. That mission is why he has a scar on his right shoulder." Stella looked away for a moment. "He took a bullet for me."

Marcus sat still, trying to process everything. As a kid, he'd asked his dad about his scars. The answers given were evasive or, at times, humorous, as Dad would say he had fought off a dinosaur or rhinoceros or was attacked by baby sharks. Once Marcus got older, he knew they were bullet or knife wounds. He loved his dad, and knowing he was a true-life hero made him love him even more.

Marcus got back to his feet. "Thank you for letting me know."

"When you call him, please tell him DragonSlayer said hello."

"I will do that. Thanks, Stella."

Marcus left and went back to his apartment. Taking his phone, he texted Olivia, apologizing for not reaching out sooner. After that, he placed the call to his hero dad.

Chapter 24

She'd never had so much fun dating, but Olivia didn't know how much longer she could stand it. She glanced at the calendar on the bakery wall. They had made it another month without going over a PG-13 rating.

They'd even celebrated Thanksgiving together. Since Marcus's parents were overseas and Alexa and Tony spent the day with Tony's family, Marcus joined Olivia's family. Even though he knew everyone, since he had lived in town longer than she had, he was pretty overwhelmed. Twenty family members and Chester and Maybelline had gathered around Aunt Katherine's big dining table. The little kids had their table, and even the dogs, Filbert and Filbertina, were given special doggy food in a little area by themselves.

For the last two weeks, Marcus and Olivia had tried to limit their alone time as much as possible. But still, the sparks flew whenever they were around one another. Olivia sighed. Maybe she should ask Marcus to marry her, make an honest woman out of her or something like that, and put her out of her misery. Mentioning misery and marriage together probably wouldn't be a good idea. It didn't matter anyway; she would have to wait and hope things would progress to the point that he would want to marry her.

But what if Marcus didn't ask her? The thought made her heart curl in on itself and cry.

"Are you okay?"

Olivia turned to Jennifer, who had somehow snuck in and was standing beside her. "Yeah, sure. Just thinking."

"How's the decorating going?" Jennifer peered over her shoulder at the half-decorated cake.

"Good. I should be finished soon." At least, she hoped so if she could corral her wayward thoughts.

"With Christmas coming, we have lots of orders to finish. I love the holidays. We have so much to be thankful for, don't we?"

"Yes, we do," Olivia said. "I wish instead of focusing on negative things, I had been more thankful for my many blessings. I think my life would have turned out very differently."

"My husband said if he could go back and do his life over again, he would have to start as soon as he was born."

Olivia chuckled. "Surely not."

"It's true. Seth was wild. Mr. Chester is the one who led him to Christ."

"Chester?"

Jennifer grinned. "Yes. he was Seth's commanding officer in the military."

Olivia shook her head. "The longer I live in Crawdad Beach, the more I discover interesting tidbits. I would never have guessed Seth was anything but a humble, sweet man. As for Chester? I shouldn't ever be surprised by anything he's done."

"Lots going on behind the scenes in the lives of the Crawdad Beach people." Jennifer grinned as she picked up a tray of cookies. "I'll help you after closing time. I'll be out front if you need me."

"Thanks, Jennifer."

Olivia glanced at the clock. She needed to hurry. Marcus was picking her up at five thirty to take them to dinner and then to a pottery class. Olivia hoped her skill level had improved from the last time she tried to make something out of clay. She'd taken a class when she was twelve, and her bowl-making attempt looked more like a squatty ashtray. Her poor, non-smoking dad had acted ridiculously thankful to receive her gift.

Olivia chuckled, then sucked in a breath. She hadn't gotten upset when she thought about her dad. The memory just made her smile.

Driving back to Crawdad Beach, Marcus was still ticked off about the pottery teacher's flirting with Olivia. Even another guy named Tom had shown her way too much attention. She hadn't seemed to notice, but boy Marcus did. Greg, the pottery teacher, had stood behind Olivia, his arms around hers, showing her how to work with the clay. Marcus felt the anger rising again just thinking about it.

Her bowl had come out perfect, but his rebellious, stubborn clay had fought him no matter what he tried. He'd wound up with something that looked like a two-year-old had made.

Olivia put lip gloss on her lips. "Greg said I really had a talent for making pottery, and he offered to give me a private lesson for a more advanced course."

Marcus tried not to growl. "He did, did he? That was nice of Greg." Didn't Olivia notice what a jerk that guy had been? How he flirted with her while her boyfriend was with her?

"What's wrong?" Olivia looked over at him. "Didn't you have fun?"

Trying to act more upbeat, Marcus smiled her way. "Sure. It was great."

She tilted her head for a moment, then shrugged. "I loved it. This was the first time I've ever been able to make something that looked good. I can't wait to try again. I might go over on Saturday and get a private lesson. Tom said he might be there too."

Marcus gripped the steering wheel until his knuckles went white. Both guys wanted to be there with Olivia.

There was no way Marcus would let her be alone with the flirtatious jerks. "I could drive you."

"No, that's okay. I can go by myself. I know you didn't have a very good time." Olivia continued talking about what she would make next, how excited she was, how nice Greg and Tom had been, and on and on and on about pottery and how great it was.

Marcus clenched his teeth so hard his jaw throbbed in pain. He had been an idiot in suggesting that they take the class.

When they arrived at her building, since it was late, he walked her to her door.

She wrapped her arms around him. "I had such a great time."

He held her against him. "I love you, Olivia."

"I love you too." She tilted her head up to kiss him. "See you tomorrow?"

"I'm here to stay."

She smiled. "Good." One more quick kiss, she opened her door and locked it behind her.

Marcus stood on the sidewalk. Dating like this couldn't go on. Trying to avoid being alone together stunk because he wanted to be alone with Olivia. And there was no way he was going to keep taking her places where predators were hanging around.

It wasn't like he had a claim on Olivia, but he couldn't take a chance on losing her to another guy. No, he needed to take action.

Marcus checked the time and groaned. It was too late. He'd have to wait until tomorrow. Making a mental list of what he needed to do, he walked back to his apartment.

Chapter 25

Olivia locked the bakery door. The day's sales had been great, but she hadn't heard from Marcus all day. She'd checked her phone a zillion times, but nothing. Not a missed call. Not even a text.

The more she thought about last night's pottery class, the worse she felt. Marcus hadn't had a good time, and she had been all chatty about her great time.

She trudged up the stairs and crashed on the couch. Drawing her legs up, she wrapped her arms around them. Was Marcus busy, or had she done something wrong? Maybe she enjoyed Greg and Tom's attention a little too much.

Olivia nibbled on her lip. When she asked Marcus last night if she would see him, he said he was here to stay. Which was a good statement, but he didn't say he would see her.

What if he didn't want to be with her anymore? She couldn't let that happen. She loved him, and he loved her. Marcus was not going to get away. She needed to get ready in case he called and wanted to take her out.

Olivia jumped to her feet. Better yet, she should cook

a mouth-watering meal, shower, dress in something sexy but not too sexy, and show up at his door.

Marcus groaned. He'd stayed so busy time had gotten away from him. He should have contacted Olivia before now.

Grabbing his phone, he called her number. It rang and went to voicemail. Was she not home? Was she mad at him? He was a jerk about the other guys flirting and even her excitement over the pottery class.

Marcus blew out a breath. He should have been happy for her with how great she did at making pottery. It wasn't like Olivia had been the one flirting. It wasn't her fault that she was beautiful and would draw attention wherever she went.

He tried Olivia's number again. Still no answer. He texted her, but the message said it failed. Was something wrong? What if something had happened to her? He paced in his office. Olivia was a single woman living alone in a big building. He'd always considered Crawdad Beach a safe little town until that incident with Stella.

Maybe he could go bang on Olivia's door. Would she even hear him if she was in her apartment? If only he had a key, he could go in and make sure she was okay. He snapped his fingers. That's what he needed to do: drive to

Jennifer's house and pick up the key. He looked around the apartment again to ensure everything was ready, then ran to get his car.

Thirty minutes later, with key in hand, he unlocked the back door of Olivia's building and stepped inside. In the darkness, a light came from the stairway. He tried Olivia's phone again, but there was still no answer.

Was someone holding her hostage? Why didn't he bring his gun? After what happened with Stella, he shouldn't take chances. He should have warned Olivia to always be careful.

Should he call out? No. If someone was there, that might make things worse. Marcus crept forward. A creaky stair made him cringe. He paused. From Olivia's apartment, he heard a loud thump. Oh, no.

He couldn't wait; he needed to get up there and make sure she was okay. Racing up the final stairs, he grabbed the door, opened it, stepped inside, and started to call her name.

Whap!

Blackness filled his vision, and he crumpled to the floor.

"Marcus?" Olivia's voice came from far away.

Was she crying? Why was his head spinning? Why did his nose hurt so bad? He groaned and tried to open his eyes.

"I'm so sorry. Please talk to me. Marcus, I love you.

Please be okay."

It took all his strength to finally get an eye open. Everything was fuzzy. Was that Olivia's beautiful face hovering above him? Had he died and gone to heaven? He attempted a smile. Was he drooling? Why was she holding a bat?

Marcus struggled to get on his feet. The world tilted, and the hardwood floor met his face.

Olivia's scream jolted him to reality.

Groaning, he rolled over and stared at the ceiling. He touched his face. Was his nose broken? Was he bleeding? Where were his glasses?

Olivia's shaky hand put them on him, and her beautiful face came into his vision. "I'm so sorry." She pushed a tissue against his nose. "I didn't know it was you." Her bottom lip wobbled as her tears fell on his face. "I would never hit you."

Realization dawned. Olivia had hit him with a bat. Obviously, he should have let her know it was him creeping up the stairs. At least she was safe. Marcus chuckled.

Olivia's expression changed. "You're laughing. Did you do that on purpose?" She raised the weapon.

"No!" He kept the tissue on his nose as he held up his other hand. He struggled to get on his feet. "I thought something had happened to you. I tried to call, but you never answered."

"You did *not* call. I checked my phone a million times, a gazillion times, and there was not one message from you."

Even though his face throbbed in pain, he grinned. Even angry, she looked beautiful. He'd never seen that dress before. It hugged her gorgeous curves, and she smelled so good.

"It's not funny, Marcus Patterson." Still holding the bat, Olivia crossed to the other side of the room, picked up her phone, and held it toward him. "See, not one message."

Marcus stared at the black screen. "Is your phone dead?"

Olivia jerked it back toward her, and her face went crimson. "Oh no. I'm so sorry. The battery must have gone dead because I checked it so much." She ran to him and hugged him. "I'm so sorry."

Still holding the tissue against his throbbing nose, he put an arm around her. His face might be broken in two, but how he loved this woman.

Chapter 26

Why couldn't she just disappear? She'd hit Marcus in the face. With. A. Bat. What if she broke the nose of the man she loved? What if she gave him brain damage?

She squirmed out of his embrace and checked his face. "Are you okay? Is your nose broken? How is your head? Are you thinking okay?"

"I'm sure I'll be fine. At least I know you can take care of yourself. I'm very sorry for scaring you." He looked at the bloody tissue. "I think the bleeding has stopped."

She hugged him again. "I'm glad you're okay."

"Me too." He tipped her face up toward his. "You look beautiful. Would you be so kind to escort me back to my apartment?"

"Yes, I'm sure you need to sit down and rest. I made dinner. I can bring it with me, and you can just take it easy, okay?"

"I'll stand right here and wait for you." He leaned against the wall.

Olivia hurried to the kitchen, grabbed her delivery bag, put the dishes inside, and ran back to Marcus.

Marcus draped an arm across her shoulder. "I might

need a little help down the stairs."

"Right. Yes, just hold onto me."

Olivia held the delivery bag in one hand and kept a tight grip on Marcus to make sure he wouldn't pass out.

Once they arrived at his apartment, he gave her the door key. Inside, she led him to the couch. A fire in his fireplace cast a warm glow across the room.

After Marcus settled, she went to the kitchen and put the delivery bag on the counter. She needed to ensure he ate something and keep him awake all night. Wasn't that what you were supposed to do when someone passed out? Or was that for a concussion?

Did he have a concussion? There was no way Olivia would do an internet search on how to treat someone hit in the face with a baseball bat.

She stepped back into the den. Marcus wasn't there. Should she be worried? Maybe he needed to visit the bathroom and fix his nose. Would they have to break it if it was broken to make it okay? It wasn't tilted when she looked at it, so maybe it would be okay.

This was not the evening she'd planned. She wanted to surprise Marcus with a delicious meal and a wonderful PG-13 evening. Instead, she'd smashed his face.

She sat up and listened. Did she hear soft music?

Marcus, carrying a vase of roses, walked toward her. "Flowers for my lady." He set them on the coffee table.

"How sweet. Thank you. They're beautiful." Her

bottom lip trembled. "I don't deserve flowers after what I did to you."

Trying to keep his hands steady, Marcus reached into his pocket and took a deep breath. "I love you, Olivia Baker."

He knelt on one knee and held out the open small velvet box. Inside was the marquis-cut diamond ring his cousins had helped him choose.

"Will you marry me?"

Olivia's face looked like it would crack. She let out a loud wail. Sobbing, she put her face in her hands.

Marcus felt the blood drain from his face to his toes. This is not the way he thought she would respond. Talk about a blow to the ego. He'd never asked anyone to marry him before. What was he supposed to do now?

Getting off his knees, he sat beside her and patted her shoulder.

She collapsed against him and kept crying.

Thank goodness he hadn't recorded the occasion.

Wide-eyed, Olivia looked at him and said something, but her words didn't make sense. All he could make out was his name and then blubbering, sobbing something.

She held up her hand and gulped down more sobs.

Now, he wished her bat had hit him harder and

knocked him out for good. This had to be the most embarrassing moment of his life. He'd asked the woman he loved to marry him, and all she could do was cry.

Looking slightly crazy, Olivia grabbed his shirt. "I don't deserve you. How could you want to marry me?" Another sob. Tears running down her cheeks, and her lip still trembling, she took a deep breath. "Yes, I'll marry you." She vaulted in his arms and kissed him like he hoped she would kiss him forever.

Chapter 27

Olivia wiggled her toes in the warm white sand as she stared at the crystal-clear ocean. Why was God so kind to her? She didn't deserve His forgiveness and the many blessings He had given her. When she finally released her anger, shame, and guilt, she found God's love waiting. And God's love was beyond anything she could have ever imagined. Looking at the blue sky, she thanked God again and again and again.

Marcus's strong arms wrapped around her, and he kissed the top of her head. "Happy?"

"I'm more than happy." She leaned against his chest. "This is the best honeymoon ever." The ten days they'd spent together were even better than she had imagined. Loving someone when it was right and good in God's eyes was incredibly wonderful. "Thank you for marrying me."

"Thank you. Once we were engaged, waiting those four months to marry you was the hardest thing I've ever done."

Olivia turned toward him and gave him an apologetic look. "I know. I'm sorry that I wanted a spring wedding. We should have eloped."

"That would have been nice. With all the cold showers I had to take, my skin was starting to look like a prune."

She giggled. "I don't think you'll have to worry about that again."

His grin made her heart happy dance. She wanted to pinch herself to make sure she wasn't dreaming. She was married to a wonderful man, and his parents had welcomed her into their family with smiles and open arms.

"Are you enjoying Puerto Vallarta?"

"I love it here. Of course, I would have been happy wherever we went since we're together."

He kissed her in ways that promised the evening activities would again be extremely enjoyable.

A little dazed, she grinned at her handsome husband. "Thank you. I do hope that is a preview of later attractions."

"You can count on that. So, what do you think of my grandparent's home?"

"It's beautiful. I can't believe you have a private beach and a villa. I see why you enjoyed coming here."

"Now that we're married, we have a villa and a private beach anytime we want to visit. How about we go to town and get some dinner?"

"Anywhere you take me, I'll be happy."

While Olivia finished getting ready, Marcus stood at the window in the master suite and stared at the ocean.

He'd always loved his grandparent's villa. The memories he and Olivia shared here added to his joy. Maybe someday they would bring their children here to visit. Not that he wanted to rush into having a family. He wanted as much time as possible to have Olivia all to himself.

Since this was their last honeymoon night, he planned on spoiling his new wife with a five-star meal from the finest restaurant in the city.

Marcus finished dressing and checked his phone. A message from Stella raised his eyebrows. *"Be careful when you return to Crawdad Beach."*

The End

of *A Baker's Heart*
and the beginning of
Marcus and Olivia's lives together.

Find out more in the next book in the series!

Thank you for reading,

A Baker's Heart

To the Reader

Thank you for taking the time to read *A Baker's Heart.* Olivia's story is like that of many who struggle to trust God after life's difficulties. Hardship makes us wonder where God is and why he doesn't fix everything and answer all our prayers.

Pain, illness, and death will continue in this broken world until time ends. However, no matter what adversity we face, God is still good, and His loving arms are open to all who will come to Him. May your story also read that you found God's love.

If you liked the book, would you be so kind as to leave a positive review and/or tell your friends? As an author, hearing someone enjoyed my stories makes the long hours of living in a fictional world worth every minute.

For every review given, the Crawdadians of Crawdad Beach will send their thanks, and Olivia will bake you a no-calorie, yummy imaginary dessert.

Acknowledgments

To my loving Heavenly Father, thank You for the stories You bless me to write.

My sweet husband, Dennis, thank you for loving me even when I spend hours and hours hanging out with imaginary people in imaginary towns.

Patricia (PacJac) Carroll, thank you for your friendship and the fun ways you motivate me to continue writing.

Jack Foster, thank you again for the creative Crawdad drawings I've used throughout the Crawdad Beach Series. Readers, please visit Jack at jackfosterart.com

About the Author

Lisa Buffaloe is a happily married mom, multi-published author, and speaker. When Lisa's not writing, she enjoys spending time with God, gardening, walking with her husband, and exploring God's beautiful nature. Visit Lisa at https://lisabuffaloe.com

Books by Lisa
Fiction
A Baker's Heart
Crystal's Journey Home
Visible, yet Hidden
Running to Grace
The Masterpiece Beneath
Nadia's Hope
Prodigal Nights
Writing Her Heart
The Discovery Chapter
Open Lens
The Fortune
Grace for the Char-Baked

Non-Fiction
Float by Faith
Heart and Soul Medication
Time with The Timeless One

The Forgotten Resting Place
Present in His Presence
We Were Meant for Paradise
One Lit Step: Devotions for your journey
The Unnamed Devotional
Flying on His Wings
Unfailing Treasures
No Wound Too Deep For The Deep Love of Christ
Living Joyfully Free Devotional (Volumes 1 & 2)

A Baker's Heart

Lisa Buffaloe

www.ingramcontent.com/pod-product-compliance
Lightning Source LLC
Chambersburg PA
CBHW071240130626
46556CB00003B/1096